OUT OF PLACE

'This has got movie written all over it.'

Denis Walter, 3AW, Sydney

'Richly researched, splendidly illuminating. *A Break in the Chain* offers insider history, the private story beyond the public history, an emotionally dense and intriguing Australian story of high achievement, and of cultures and traditions in rich conflict.'

Writer and academic Michael Meehan

FOR WOMEN WHO GRIEVE

'Tansley's warm personal disclosures will undoubtedly assist women who mourn; those who feel lost and dejected will find joy and hope in place of despair, and a sense of purpose for the future.'

Canberra Times

'…the clear message from one grieving woman to others is that "you are not alone" and that "your experience is valued and normal"…'

Australian Health Review

'…an essential and valuable addition to any collection of "help" books on the painful and sensitive subject of death, dying, and the process of grieving.'

Midwest Book Review

'…this is a sensible, sensitive approach to the grieving process that would be as helpful to a man as to a woman whose spouse has died…'

Fifty-Plus

'This book is written in the form of a series of steps to take the reader gently through different stages of grief — understanding death, letting go, being gentle with yourself, world of words, dreaming, mind control…'

Weekly Times (Vic)

OUT OF PLACE

TANGEA TANSLEY

First published in 2014

This is a work of fiction. Names and characters are the products of the author's imagination and any resemblance to actual persons, living or dead, is entirely coincidental.

Published by That's Entertaining, Perth, Western Australia.

National Library of Australia Cataloguing-in-Publication entry
Author: Tansley, Tangea, 1948- author.
Title: Out of Place / Tangea Tansley.
ISBN: 9780994162526 (paperback)
Dewey Number: A823.4

p.1: Quotation from a written work by artist Leonie Watston
p.100: Quotation from *A Rage to Live* by Mary S. Lovell, Abacus, 1999, p. 133.

Cover: Su Halfwerk/Novel Prevue based on the original ebook cover by Rita Toews
Cover photograph: Piskunov/iStock
Author photograph backcover: Richard Wheater

For Richard

'Tis all a Chequer-board of Nights and Days
Where Destiny with Men for Pieces plays
Hither and thither moves, and mates, and slays,
And one by one back in the Closet lays.

THE RUBAIYAT OF OMAR KHAYYAM XLIX

PROLOGUE

London 1995

Inside painting
there are hidden histories
of desire and repulsion...

It had taken him almost as long to finish this painting as it had to start it in the first place. Just why that was he didn't care to explore. It was enough, almost enough, to sit in front of this beach scene that he had committed at last to canvas, to keep working up the perspective of the littoral, so that the retreating water still gleamed on the sand, so the glassy bubbles of air that led down to the caves of the hermit crabs showed here and there, a shining inner beach that joined the sandy shore and led downwards to the waves foaming one on top of the other, hunkering at the border until they had gained enough strength to run back up the beach to stop just short of the last line in the sand that he'd marked with scraps of seaweed, the soft pinks and greys of shell grit.

He had it almost right, he thought. This in-between stretch, this linking and separating of two worlds. Into this gap was built all the time in the world which was never enough. Into it he'd painted his memories of an endless space of sand that had looked at first as if it would stretch forever until you entered the tall gates, until you took four paces to come up short with your nose against the roughcast concrete wall. For him, the compound in the desert had been just another place. But for her?

He shook his head. Impossible for his conscious mind to know. But then perhaps he still didn't quite want to know. Perhaps this link was as far as he could go. Her sandals hanging from one hand. The soft wrap of her skirt moving with the swing of her hips. In this painting he had made the dry and hopeless sand filmy wet because that was how it had looked to him the day she walked away.

He had in his hand a brush so fine it might have been chosen by the ancient calligraphers. Without taking his eyes from his work, he sucked lightly on the bristles, smoothed them to a sharp point with the rag in his other hand. He had finished with the sand for now, with the range of pale sepia blobs of oil paint he had mixed with Egyptian white or cream on the dinner plate at his elbow. It seemed right, somehow, that this ink of cuttlefish should end up back where it started – on a seashore.

But now he was ready to write with the brush in a shade of royal blue, his hand moving surely and quickly in what was almost a copperplate script, tracing over his pencil lines to write a message more permanent. To give the work a name. He had been working on the mount laid on the counter-top of his desk to one side of the canvas, a creamy board he had decorated with scrolls and minarets in pale browns and light blues that complemented the painting, that lent it, he fancied, something of the Middle East in which it was set. In a departure from his usual practice, he had decided to place the title in a scroll on the mount itself and it was this he was working on with his finest bristle brush.

'Almost finished, is it then?' The voice of his wife suddenly at his elbow with the tea tray held shoulder-high startled him. Neither of them had thought to put a small table outside the door to assist with this daily ritual – or perhaps it was that they thought about it often, but did nothing – so usually there was a short scuffle outside the door as she balanced the tray on her raised knee in order to free one hand for long enough to turn the knob.

Usually he was given enough warning, but today she was by his side before he realized she was in the room. It was not that the painting itself had to be hidden. Not that anything had to be hidden, really. Just something in himself that had to be realigned, a correction, quite small like the adjustment of one's clothing, but in terms of one's personal comfort, or pride, important nonetheless.

He jerked around, wanting to throw the cloth over the oil, resisting the pull in himself to do so, settling instead for his usual self-mocking expression. Mask enough. He gave a half-shrug as she rattled a place for the tray among the tools of his work. She busied herself with a stir for the pot, a sugar cube for each cup and a shot of milk before lifting the teapot high and pouring it in such a way that the fragrance of the tea cut through the oily air to blend with the milk and sugar to give off an altogether different aroma. She placed two ginger nut biscuits on each of the saucers.

'There. There you are.' Pulling a chair towards him, she passed him his tea before she settled herself opposite, her own cup on her knee, frowning as she faced the window. 'Winter coming early this year. It's almost dark outside already. Chilly, too. I'm surprised you don't die your death in here.'

He hadn't noticed. The light in this attic room he used as his studio was generally good, the windows south-facing and sufficiently large to gather in any available daylight and warmth. But then his style of painting was so fine and – quite suddenly – his eyes no longer so good that he'd gone to some expense to get a strong light set up over his easel and another over the counter that he used for mixing paint and colour, and both bulbs tended to emit heat. At some point in the day, he would get up to turn on one or other of these lights, but it was seldom a conscious decision, just something he did when it was required of him, when he became aware of the lack of distinction in the tones at his elbow.

He got up to switch off the light over the easel, surprising himself at how it changed the scene. Made the figure in his painting gloomily distant as she walked away from him over the shining sand. As if he had set her on this path with her head up and looking into the future, set her quite deliberately on a course that led step by step across the rippling sand and away from him. He noticed now what he hadn't been conscious of creating: the set of her shoulders that suggested determination, the thrust of her hip that told him she was aware he was watching. Wanted him still to watch.

With the same closeness about him, he sat again to take up his tea, burning his lips before setting it down again.

She leaned towards the work, her eyes scanning the words he had just written.

'Don't have my glasses and now you've gone and made it gloomier still in here. What's that you've written? *To my darling?* Is that it? Is that what it says, Taylor? *To my darling.* Very romantic of you. I must say Taylor luv.' She sat back. 'You don't normally title your work on the actual work itself.'

She had the hint of a smile about her mouth, but it was about as reassuring as a dog that wags its tail stiff and high on meeting a strange dog. Although quite some considerable portion of their married years had been spent apart, all up they numbered nearly fifty and he knew her well enough to pick up on the tension in her last sentence. He shrugged, smiled it away with a downward twist of his lips.

'Uh. For want of a title. . . Had to say somethin'. What do you think? Help its chances of a quick sale?'

What games we play, he thought. I hate this. I hate the discussion of a work before it's complete, its public display before it's ready. Held up uncloaked. He knew he should cover the canvas. But he knew also that he couldn't and wouldn't, but would sit and pretend he didn't care.

'It's pretty enough anyway, I think,' she said. 'In fact, I think I like what you've done with this one. It looks like an eighty-mile beach you've got there. And I like the way you've got the girl walking into the never-never. It's got a forever look about it. The way you've done that beach. It'll sell regardless. I'm sure it will.' Her face relaxed. 'For one taking it up so late and all, I must say you've got . . . Well you've got a certain knack.'

Turning her back on the painting, she went on to talk about the new hot water system she wanted and he drew a breath and readily talked through the quotations she had gathered, the merits of one plumber over another, the current unreliability of all tradesmen and when had it been any different? After all? When they finished, she gathered up the cups, tipped the dregs of one into the other, stacked them on the tray.

'Don't work too late,' she said as she repeated the procedure of coming in. Moving out through the door, balancing the tray, pulling the door closed behind her. It was like a family movie. Winding in. Rolling out.

Taylor sagged in his high chair until the latch caught. And then he bent to one side, caught at the night cloth with which he normally draped his works and slung it over the painting.

Mary was right. It *was* cold in here, and dark, too, with the dusk nearly done. Breathing deeply, he folded his arms across his chest, gazing at the splattered cloth that faced him through the gloom. Willed his mind not to think about the figure walking away from him along a road he was unable, and unwilling, to share. And at the same time flattered, scared too, knowing that he was the one who held the cards. He didn't need to lift the cloth to know that she looked lost, but bravely so. Something about her that suggested an attempt at nonchalance which didn't quite come off. Like pulling on a garment suddenly outgrown. Was that something he had imagined or had it been so? Now that his artwork had taken over from the real it was impossible to tell. Impossible, too, that an image could stay with him for nearly half a lifetime. For something like thirty years or more. What had they talked about back then? He'd been so full of himself. Cocksure bastard.

He had hoped that in painting this picture, finding finally inside himself whatever it took to set it down – which was not courage exactly, because how could it be when it was a move to erase the memory of his own cowardice? – would have a similar result to telling a story. That once it was done, once he had set down the tale for all to see, once he had held the essence of his memory up to the light and given it its own reality, that the past would let him alone and that he would be able move on. But, so far, that was proving not to be the case.

ONE

Thirty years earlier

The aerogramme she grips in both hands is no different from the others, but in the minutes before she opens it, she knows she has run out of time.

Leaving the dark rainy evening behind her, Dana slides the bolt on the inside of the door. She shrugs off her raincoat, glances briefly into the mirror of the hallstand as she passes. But today something stops her so she steps back on one heel to try to find some remnant of the person she knows – or thinks she knows – in the curiously lifeless image that stares back at her. Like a ghost, she thinks. But a ghost from the future.

She stands her briefcase between her feet, runs one hand through her dark hair limp with the damp, makes a face at the silvered glass, at this woman with her eyebrows drawn tight and her mouth set – the lipstick of the morning long since defeated by the day. She could do with a haircut, but it's deeper than that. Maybe Dekker's right, maybe she does take the job too seriously. Maybe she takes everything too seriously.

Still standing in the hall, she closes her eyes, takes a deep breath as she slides a fingernail into the small gap under the flap, slits it along the fold and glances at the date. As usual it has taken six weeks to get here, the length it's been in transit always sets up a feeling of anxiety in her. She knows that if anything serious happened, he would be in touch by telegram. But, still, it's a fair amount of time to wait. Anything can happen in six weeks.

So she skips to the end first, the last paragraph on the back page in her husband's generously looping script…*so I say to you, come prepared to love this place. That's the only way this will work, Dana. So much to see and nothing to do but enjoy yourself for six months or a year. Or longer if you wish… Heh! You must come soon, girl. Very soon!*

This is the moment – standing in front of the mirror in the dim hallway – that she recognises the resolution lodged already in her subconscious. I do look tired, she tells her slumping shoulders. But then, as if in protest, they lift and straighten. She sighs. Increasingly these days she catches herself addressing an empty room. And after all, why the hesitation anyway? Nothing's forever. Is it?

In the kitchen she pulls the cork on a bottle of wine, pours herself a glass and opens the fridge door to gaze at its empty shelves. She settles for a handful of cashews, takes a generous gulp of her drink and reaches for the phone.

When her mother-in-law's voice comes over the wire three rings later, she doesn't give herself time to back out.

'I'm going,' she says through a mouthful of nuts. 'Just as soon as I can get everything together, I'll be joining

Dekker.' Holds the phone away from her ear at the gleeful squeal.

'I knew it! When you were ready, I knew you would go.'

Dana takes another sip of wine, settles into a chair and listens through to the end of her glass at her mother-in-law's exclamations of open delight. She can certainly talk, but then that's Monica Malan – a warm grey-haired woman it's difficult not to like. It's typical that she has put no pressure on Dana over these last months. In fact, in a guilty sort of way, Dana finds herself closer to her mother-in-law than her own mother. It's not that she doesn't love her mother, but she finds her somehow indistinct, an extension of her father. Her parents' marriage is one of those, she supposes, where one plus one equals less than two.

'I say, I don't suppose you can find the time to pop down and see us before you leave?' Maybe, Dana says. She'll certainly try. She has to give four weeks' leave at the museum, let the flat – and so forth.

'That might not be so easy – to give up the job, that is. I know how much you love it.' Monica says. 'But hang in there. It'll all be worth it. And we're not far away if you need us.'

But she *is* far away, Dana thinks when the call finishes and she hangs up. Dekker's parents live on a property in Constantia down in the Cape, more than half a country away from Johannesburg. Sometimes she's wished them closer, but perhaps the success of their relationship is predicated on its remaining just the way it is.

She sits for a moment wondering about the *and so forth*. What exactly does she have to do first? The visa has been arranged for ages, so fortunately she does not have to worry about that. She will need vaccinations of some description, but that is easy enough and it's not as if they have children to organise, pets to foster out.

Just the flat to do something with really. Dekker likes to call it an apartment, but while it's comfortable and it's home, she's never thought of it as other than an easy-care two-bedroom flat with a balcony that looks out onto an equally pleasant park. Perhaps she should let it? Six months or a year? Fully furnished? She can picture the ad in the *Star*'s Classifieds – *Suit professional couple, ten minutes from the city...* From what Dekker has said, it doesn't sound as though money is going to be a problem – at least for the foreseeable future. But surely she can't just walk out and close the door?

This is something she would like to talk through with her husband, a decision he should be part of, but the mail will take too long and calling him is impossible. As yet, there is no telephone on site he tells her and there's no knowing when, or even if, a line will be connected. The one time he called he'd had to travel to some sort of a postal outlet which, she gathered from his tone of annoyance, was some way away and where he'd had to wait his turn. Stand in line for an hour in return for the few minutes of doubtful communication while they tried to converse on the crackling line – each finding they had to wait for the echo of their voices to die away before the other spoke. But it had been good to hear his voice.

She gets up to pour herself another glass of wine, finds a pad and pencil to start making a list of what she has to do. The point of no return rears like a beacon in front of her. I'm actually going, she tells herself.

It's been almost six months since she came home to find Dekker, champagne bottle in hand, cork popping as she walked into the room. His face was glowing.

'BESA's won the tender to build a commercial port in the Gulf. The Persian Gulf. I'm the only one going from the South African division and they picked me because of my marine experience on the Californian sub base. Whoo!' He swung across to drop a kiss on her cheek.

She dropped her bag onto the sofa and took the glass he handed to her. Slung herself into a chair.

'Gosh,' she said as their glasses touched. 'Congratulations. When?'

'Soon. Soon as they can get the visa and paperwork in place. Let me tell you.' He gave her shoulder a squeeze and propped himself on the arm of the chair beside her. 'Al-Khasi is the place. Just here. See.' He bent over the atlas he had open on the coffee table, his finger pressing into a space half land, half sea. 'Only a fishing village at the moment. Right on the edge of the Gulf. But we'll live on the Brit compound just a little way out. I'll go out first. That'll give me time to suss out the joint and you can take your time finishing up here. If they know you're coming out within a couple of months, say, they'll give me a family house – beats single quarters – and I can set things up for you. Smooth the path.' He rubs his hands together.

'But – my job, Dekker. What about the job?'

'Give it up, my girl. No problem about that. But I haven't told you everything yet. Because now, you see, you no longer have to work. It will no longer be necessary. You know what they'll pay me for this, eh? Twenty thousand a year! Sterling, that is. No tax! Totally tax-free. So, you see, you can relax. Do exactly what you want. And then perhaps…' He raised his glass to her and as he took a sip he looked at her pointedly, raised his eyebrows rapidly once, twice. He squeezed her shoulder again. 'Don't look so worried, Dana. It's not as though we didn't know it was on the cards. Smile.'

She had tried for a happy face, but it occurred to her for the first time how like her father Dekker was in his focused planning. In the short time that had elapsed between being offered the contract and telling her, he had it all worked out. But she had found it difficult to match his enthusiasm and, following his departure, the couple of months had ballooned out. It wasn't that she *didn't* want to go, but she was not sure she did, either.

But it is plain she can prevaricate no longer. The car, too, she thinks now. I'll have to do something about the car. And packing. A couple of tea-chests have gone ahead by sea. What else will she need? Something to do while she's there. Painting? She might try once again to paint. Or draw. *It's imperative that I work while I'm there, she says to the room. At least two paintings…or the start of a series of drawings perhaps…two good works must result from this time. I promise myself…I promise.* Which reminds her of her father. She will have to call her parents.

And Dekker – she could try a telegram. The list gets longer. And the museum. Tomorrow. Tomorrow's the day she will have to put in her notice.

TWO

Now, just over four weeks later, she is folded into the window seat of a DC-9. The plane is rocking and she feels slightly sick as she reaches for the blue aerogramme, smoothes it out one more time. She has handled it so often that it is furring along the folds, threatening to tear along the seam that has been written across in Dekker's strong hand. Nothing since, but there could be any number of reasons for that.

What had finally triggered her decision is still not quite clear to her. It was more, surely, than her tired reflection staring back at her at the end of a working day. In part she has missed Dekker over the past few months, but if she were asked what exactly she missed and why, she isn't sure she would know the answer. Perhaps it's as simple as the Christmas trees that have been progressively appearing in shop windows provoking thoughts of how he would manage alone in the desert during this time of family celebration. Which was all part of an earlier unrelated guilt surfacing again: the realization she was letting everyone down by her obstinacy in remaining in one place when her role as a wife was clearly in another. Or perhaps it was simply the degree of inevitability that was there all the time, so once she'd made the decision everything fitted together so easily she wondered why she hadn't made it sooner.

She flips the flimsy paper closed, places it this time in the side flap of the bag squashed into the seat pocket in front of her, picks up her book. But her husband's phrases dance over the words on the page, his strong Afrikaans accent forming a refrain every bit as maddening as the lyrics of a song that keep repeating. The two faces of Dekker. *That is the only way this will work. You must come soon…* Plea or dictum? In an earlier letter, he had suggested she ask for a sabbatical from the museum. *You've been there over six years now. Surely they can tweak the system enough to allow you some months off. Or even leave without pay? Eh? Try them.*

She had tried. Approached the employment officer. 'But a sabbatical is seven years — and seven years is seven years, Dana. If we bend the rules for one… No, no. It makes it too difficult. Precedents. Don't you see?'

She saw, but she also saw that there was a young girl fresh out of Wits University who wanted her job.

So now it has to work. After resigning, it has to work.

She gives up on the book, sticks it back in the seat pocket, leans her temple against the cold glass of the window. Perhaps Dekker was right in that the museum had assumed too much importance, had absorbed too much of her time…and her energy, he would sometimes add. Maybe she is ready for a rest, ready to explore, experience a new lifestyle. Perhaps she has been in a rut, a comfortable groove, but stuck all the same. A cocoon, her friend had called it. 'The world's not about to end just because you break out of your comfy cocoon for a spell. If I had that sort of opportunity, you wouldn't see me for dust.' Margot had set down her coffee cup somewhat sharply. 'What's to debate really? The silly job will still be here when you come back. Or another even better. You might even like it there. And clearly your man wants you.' Wants or needs, Dana asked herself. Wants, needs? Or even desires?

What sort of day is shaping down there below the cloud? Raining gloom? Or bright sticky heat? Racing above the cloud cover, with the bright gold of the early dawn fast-fading and the fluff of the clouds turning pink at the edges has an element of fantasy about it. Is this how her mind is going to behave over the next months – like a sieve retaining nothing and jumping from one thought to another – and if so, will she ever get it back again? What had that woman from archives said to her at the goodbye gathering? Happy retirement? She can still see the quizzical movement of the carefully crayoned eyebrows, the up-lifted glass as she raised her own in tandem.

'Oh, but I'm not retiring,' she had said quickly, forcing a smile.

'Oh? No? Really? Well, good luck all the same.' That's all her colleague had said, the skin around her eyes crinkling, her lips stretching briefly as she turned away to answer a question.

'No,' Dana had said to the empty air. 'No, I'm not. Certainly not at only twenty-nine. This is just time out. Six months, a year at the very most, that's all it is.'

Out of Place

The plane lurches; the seat belt sign flickers. The mother in the next row of seats stands abruptly, catches up the two-year-old who has been running up and down the aisle since Riyadh. Dana snaps the clasp of her belt closed and turns to look into the future.

Everything will be fine if she can stop thinking about a job that is no longer her job, if she can look forward instead of back. She knows this. She knows, too, that she must suppress a reality that struggles for its independence rather like the kid in the seat in front of her. Which is that she hadn't really wanted to leave at all because she had enjoyed every moment she had put into her work.

The cloud below is no longer the thick dumpy pillow of new day but thinning rapidly to wispy threads of white, a worn loose-woven cloth with the world below showing through. She breathes deeply, allows herself the luxury of this one truth: that there had not been one day in the past six years that she hadn't relished the moment her car wheels rumbled up and over the freeway on-ramp to reveal the city laid out before her. A Johannesburg that from that distance and in the early-morning light looked unreal, a Camelot of sugar cubes touched gold on the side presented to the rising sun. Johannesburg, the city of her birth, increasingly ugly, cruel, dangerous, but still hers.

She'd met Dekker one such morning. The car behind her had swung out to draw up beside her at the traffic lights; the driver alighted and ran around the front of his car to her own. In his hand was a bunch of freesias tied together with string, their stalks still dripping. He'd thrust them through the window and she'd grasped them in reflex, a spontaneous, almost unquestioning reaction he would provoke in her time and again.

'Here,' he said. 'I say…that is, I think you're beautiful.' He had nodded, an over-tall, too-thin figure, bending in half to look through the window. And then the tips of his ears turned pink and he only just made it back to his car as the lights changed. Embarrassed by his own initiative or by the honking cheering traffic behind them – or perhaps on both counts – he had accelerated away in the outside lane.

Amused at first, and then flattered, she'd placed the flowers in water on her office desk where they stayed until long after they might have been thrown away. It wasn't until after they'd wilted completely to splay out over the edge of the glass jar that she had noticed his business card. Dekker Malan Project Manager BESA with a telephone number. And on the back, another number with a note scribbled underneath. *Please do me the honour of calling me sometime. Dekker.*

Was this the equivalent of being picked up? The question hovered in her mind even as she lifted the receiver. Within a month they were engaged; two months later they married. It wasn't until the night before the wedding that her mother had taken her aside.

'Are you sure this is what you want?'

'Is Dekker the man I want to marry, you mean? Of course, I'm sure. Why wouldn't I be?' She remembers the incident and even after three years, the sharp tone of her own voice. But for the first time she wonders just what it was that raised her defenses that day. Was it her mother's lack of faith in her judgement or the last-minute nature of her concern when it was really too late to consider pulling out? Was her mother picking up on some ambiguity that lay deep within herself, something she hadn't acknowledged or wasn't prepared to acknowledge because there is nowhere to go with knowledge based on doubt? Or was it something else entirely? Still some remnant of resentment that lingered on her mother's part with regard to her choice of career. At least, her father was happy. When she told him he had just smiled and gone on smiling as if he had known all along that her destiny was to marry the blond and blue-eyed Afrikaner. So speedily had the marriage day approached that she never did find out just where Dekker had seen her before and what had led to his impulsive gesture of the flowers and now she has trouble trying to remember whether she had ever asked.

The landing is elastic and bumpy, the plane's wheels bumping the tarmac and soaring upwards again like a springbok in full flight. When it finally rolls to a stop, she joins in the eager gathering of belongings from the overhead lockers, the checking of seat pockets. She sits again to thumb through the plastic folder that holds her passport, visa, ticket and vaccination certificate and then wonders why her heart thumps in her throat when the documents don't instantly become available to her probing fingers. The slight delay is long enough for almost the entire plane-load to have moved from their seats to the centre aisle, and she prepares to force herself into the twitchy press of bodies who have been waiting for this moment ever since they boarded the flight twelve hours earlier.

But why force? Why does she use the word *force*? Already. Before she is properly stamped and ticketed into the country. She joins the mass movement down the clanging steps. Rather too late now to wonder whether she wants to be here, and much, much too late to start to wonder what it will be like to live in what Dekker has described as a gated compound in a place like Saudi Arabia. No point in speculating. She deserves a holiday. That was what Dekker said. Repeats it like a mantra. Trust him, she tells herself. Treat it like time out. Besides, he has been patient.

She flows with the crowd into an enormous hall-like terminal, the vaulted ceilings springing from the stocky pillars that flank the arches around the building. Her fellow passengers fan into separate streams to queue under fly-pocked signs suspended on long chains that spell out *Health* in Arabic and English. She stands blinking in the dimness which is dim only in contrast to the brightness outside that has bleached out the view beyond the pillars. She looks for Dekker, who will stand at least a head taller than the tallest in the rest of the crowd.

The health line moves quickly. In front of a low wood table, she faces an official who gazes past her left ear. 'Cholera,' he says. As she hands him the document, he flips his red-checked headdress over his shoulder, opens the yellow booklet upside down to random blankness and stamps the page with some force before he motions forward the next in line. One down, she thinks, all too easy. She looks again for Dekker, is surprised to feel a small thrill stirring in the pit of her stomach.

At immigration, she lines up in front of an empty glass cage. Twenty minutes later nothing has changed and the box remains empty, the only void in a space teeming with confusion, the roar of an approaching jet swamping for a few moments the shouting, spitting and coughing, the loud speakers stuttering helplessly through it all. Everything moving and going nowhere. The queue behind her snakes through the unruly mass, a line of people who have begun to fuss and fidget like a bunch of drunk teens at an early-morning taxi rank. Those lucky enough to have hand baggage substantial enough to hold their weight flop onto it; others drop out of line to mill about in a nervous sort of way; small children play tag in and out the crowd.

Above the din, a sudden shout. Dana twists. A woman with her case in tow has tripped an Arab moving in the opposite direction. The man gets to his feet, black eyes hard as olive pits, brushes off the skirts of his robe hissing like a warning snake. She once saw a gypsy spit, a long stream of spittle with more words inbuilt than the *Iliad*, and this man is similarly disgusted. Oblivious to the woman's apologies, he stabs at the concrete floor with his black cane, sets off with short angry steps.

The clerk arrives finally, blinking into new day and winding a filthy *ashra* about his head; the line smartens up, shuffles forward. When it's Dana's turn at the plate-glass window, the officer glances at her passport, yawns through the mostly empty pages, and then starts at the beginning again, turning the pages more slowly this time. She wills her eyes away from the sight of his bleary eyes, the chin that bristles like an echidna, the grossness of his purple lips. He pushes the document to one side.

'What's wrong? Is something not right?' She tries to smile, wonders whether her anxiety shows in her face. 'Wait,' he orders. 'You wait. There.' He waves her to one side and beckons to the next in line, so she has no choice but to move out of the way, to stand beside the glass office, looking back down the line with a plane-load of eyes staring at her. Like a child pulled out of class for some misdemeanor. She feels her face getting hot, looks away. Out past the pillars and the arches into the too-bright day.

Keep your nose clean, Dekker had warned. *This is their country and we're the guests.*

It must be the discrepancy between the outside glare and the gloom of the terminal that is making spots dance in front of her eyes. She puts on her sunglasses. Some way down the queue the little girl she remembers from the plane swings off her mother's hand. She gazes fixedly at Dana.

'What's that lady done, Mummy? Why are we waiting? I'm hot. I want to see Daddy,' she says loudly.

'I want to see Daddy, too.' The mother's reply ripples up and down the line. 'Oh boy-oh-boy, do I want to see your Daddy.'

What on earth can be wrong with the passport? Her mind flips back to her visit to Israel and the recently completed Israel Museum in Jerusalem, the highlight of her tour two years before. 'Lose the passport,' Dekker had said when she reminded him of the Israeli stamp. 'Report it missing and apply for a new one. Any association with Israel will result in instant deportation. And that goes for anything in your suitcase, too. Even a magazine with a Coke ad is a no-no because Coca-Cola is sold in Israel.' A moment of terror as she remembers this; surely in the speed of her departure she hadn't picked up the wrong one? She knows this is not the case, but she worries all the same. Or perhaps it's the visa? It has to be the visa which, after a series of delays, was issued from London in some tripartite arrangement that required Dekker's signature as well as her own. Impossible to believe that something has gone wrong, impossible not to believe it. The queue drags on in front of her…and all the while she has no option but to stand like a dummy keeping her nose clean.

Another woman similarly cut from the pack joins her. Dana spreads her hands. 'I wonder what can be wrong.' The woman shrugs. 'Happens all the time,' she says. 'Who knows? Want my advice. Just take it, honey. Nothing else you can do. Just breathe slowly and relax. Know what I'm saying? No use trying to hurry them up. They just go slower.'

Dana leans into the pillar. The mother who is going to sort out Daddy finds a colouring book in her capacious bag. She settles the child on the floor at her feet, catches Dana's gaze, grins briefly. The official has been joined by a younger man who has been doodling on a pad and staring at the cobwebby ceiling like a fledgling Rumi ever since he let himself into the box, and the first man has dropped into a sort of stupor over the passport in front of him, his eyes following the journey of a cockroach making its way from one side of the counter to the other. Is it her imagination or is it the airlessness in this open-to-the-air building that suggests to her he is smiling to himself? Certainly his lips move, balloon a little more, and it's not until the insect starts to track across the open pages that he attempts to brush it off. Another couple step up to the box and eventually, with a level of gravitas that would do justice to a chess champion, the jumbo-load of passengers is processed to dissolve into the general chaos.

There is only one more family to stamp into the country, the mother jiggling a baby who has been crying at capacity since the plane began its descent; the father smiles gamely, pitches forward just as the official flips up the palm of his hand. He waits until they return to their places as shamed as competitors jumping the starting gun, before he reaches to one side to open Dana's passport, once again flicking through it. When it becomes clear to him that whatever was wrong previously hasn't fixed itself in this interim, he turns to the clerk. A small amount of confusion. The younger Arab sets off, returns twice; there are further exchanges before he disappears altogether with the passport held aloft like a prayer book.

She glances at her watch; the hands look locked in place. The official is there and yet not there. Her hands are wet, her mouth dry. When did she last have something to drink? She swivels a half-turn around the pillar. Should she leave her post and wander to where she guesses the main exit might be? See if she can spot Dekker? Who might, for all she knows, be waiting outside. She stares hard at the fly-specks on the cage. See if he's outside? See if he knows what is happening? She feels in her bag for his letter; her fingers close around it and the paper itself provides a type of reassurance followed, almost immediately, by a flash of resentment.

The American woman sighs. 'This really is too bad. I'm not going to stand for this. I don't see how I can be expected...' Her voice gets louder; her drawl more pronounced. Another ten minutes pass like an hour. The terminal is neither filling nor emptying, and she has the feeling that it's entirely possible to mill around in this chaotic space forever. The baggage has been unloaded in piles so finding belongings is a treasure hunt amid collapsing stacks of suitcases and metal trunks, prams, brown-paper-wrapped packages and a shade umbrella.

Another plane; the building trembles and she switches her thoughts from the things she can see to those she cannot. In some ways, those that are hidden from her are clearer because they come always with attachments, a history that links. But how can you have feelings for a rough-sawn crate, a box made of splintery wood swivelling around in the air until the crane lets it down softly, tenderly, more gently than you'd set down a piece of Ming? Don't think now of the team standing around, barely able to keep the smiles off their faces as the top is prised off, as one by one the artifacts are removed, unwrapped, examined for cracks and chips, praised or laughed at for their idiosyncrasies and their personalities before being ticked off against the shipping list. Her eyes hot. Don't think…don't…

Someone nudges her. It's the woman from the Deep South. She gestures with her chin to the glass cage. The official is waving her passport.

'What was wrong,' she asks, but he merely hands it to her and waves her away.

She takes a deep breath, lets it out in small puffs and this time when she turns it's Dekker's tall body blocking the light.

'Too long,' he murmurs. 'Much, much too long. Don't do it again.' But when she turns her face up for his kiss, he is staring over her head at the pillar behind her.

Outside the day is over-bright, cloud cover shrouding the sun, holding in the heat, suspending time; a driver deals with her luggage, opens the car doors. Pushing the forced sale of the old Ford from her mind, she climbs into the back seat of a silver-grey Volvo. Dekker gets in beside her and the car moves off, driving so smoothly that it's only the roadside whipping past that shows they are moving at all.

She has started to wind down the window when Dekker leans across and places his hand lightly on hers.

'It's air-conditioned. The windows are really better off closed.'

She settles back into her seat, tells herself this is luxury, this being driven, chauffeured. And then there's Dekker, sitting tall beside her with his legs apart and his hands clasped softly between his legs, affecting an ease she wishes she could copy. Her own legs are pinned together at her knees covered by a soft buff skirt and held to one side slanting away from him, her body half-turned towards the rush of the road's edge and the slower-sliding scope of sand beyond. In a way it is a relief that the driver is watching so closely in his rear-view mirror. It gives them a reason to sit a little apart, to maintain this slight social separation until the first-date cloud that surrounds them subsides. Below the driver's line of sight, her fingers inch across the expanse of royal blue leather towards Dekker's. He pats her hand, glances sideways at her.

'Heh, man,' he says. 'Heh, it's good to have you here.' He squeezes her knee, but he too is lost for words; between them it is almost as if there is so much to say that nothing can be said. It can wait. Patience, Dana, patience. She pinches her hands together. Wait for a short while longer. Until you are both alone.

Nothing has prepared her for the first sight of the waters of the Gulf. Given the postal system, answers to many of her questions are still catching up. Sand and sea go together like bread and butter and commonsense suggests that where there is sand there might also be sea, but in all the tossing and thinking alone in the double bed, in all her cogitations about the desert, somehow a coastline didn't figure. So when the car rolls smoothly onto the coast road, her breath catches not only at the unexpectedness of it, but also at its startling beauty. Away from land, the water is the usual light and dark of moss agate, but here at the shore it is a curiously luminous shade of pale green, an endlessness of colour like a waterfall of liquid glass. Or a length of green silk sari held up to the full moon.

Puncturing the surreal feeling that has gripped her since landing, she gives a yelp. Turns to Dekker, prods him lightly in the thigh.

'Wow! How on earth do you capture that! I wouldn't know what to do first, whether to photograph it or paint it or swim in it. I've never seen anything quite so deliciously tempting. I know just where I'll be hanging out in this heat.'

Leaning to tap the driver on the shoulder, he pats her knee with the other hand. 'Here. Just here, turn right.' Twists back to her smiling. 'Steady on. Not quite so easy here. Swimming, that is. Well, not in the same way as back home. I'll explain later. But, look, here's the village. And this, this is what passes for the main street.'

The car lumbers, more like a tank than a car, as it lifts one tire at a time over the rubble path that runs through a group of buildings. Children halted in their game by the arrival of the unexpected scatter like chickens to each side of the track. She taps on the window, waves and is rewarded by the coy flickers of their hands, their faces radiant with laughter.

'Doesn't take much to excite them, does it? There's not much that happens here in the way of shopping either. As you can see. The women go to al-Dhuraf for anything major. Where you'll be able to get most things. You're luckier than most in that you'll have a driver. Most of the wives don't have access to a car. Then they're stuck with the bus.

'And this…' He points to a lopsided building standing on what appears to have become a corner solely by default by virtue of the haphazardly sited group of dwellings that stretch away at right angles on either side. 'This, so far, is the only place to get food in the village, though there's some talk of another shop being built. Most women go up to the town once a month to fill the freezer. The massive freezer we've got. Wait until you see that!'

Outside the shop there is an enormous pile of rubbish: broken bricks, bottles, tin cans, paper, cardboard boxes, rotting vegetables, fish heads. Once she's noticed one, she sees other identical heaps. Each building with its own mountain of debris. Each home with its own private rubbish dump.

'Happy cherubs,' she says of the plump cats scampering about the mound feasting in the sunshine. 'Fish bones aplenty. Of course, so close to the sea. The fish here must be gorgeous… But, Dekker?' She looks most closely. 'Do you know? I do believe those are rats? Hell. Hundreds of them. Big ones!'

He scratches the back of his neck.

'Yesterday's sunburn making itself felt. Yes, lots of them here. Big rat problem. Unfortunately, it's the way they dispose of – or, to be more accurate, *don't* dispose of – the rubbish that causes the problem. But it's not half as bad as it was six months ago. Believe me.'

He taps the driver on the shoulder and the car gathers speed out of the hamlet. From behind a barred window, just level with the ground, she sees a pair of dark eyes slide quickly backwards into the gloom. From somewhere, even through the closed car window, she thinks she hears the sound of music playing.

Minutes later, giant gateposts and then a toy town of prefabricated houses, each identical to its neighbour, each sitting in a bed of sand, each with a pathway to the front door from the tarred roads that form a grid through the compound. Do the gates close behind them? Her neck is suddenly too stiff to turn.

Dekker touches her knee again.

'Beautifully laid out, eh? They've thought of everything. You'll see. And so safe for the children. Oh…and there's a party tonight. Think you can fight off the jet lag for a couple of hours this evening? I'm throwing you in the deep end, I know, but the sooner you meet people the better.'

THREE

By the time they arrive at the Richardsons' it's already noisy and smoky, and as they walk in through the open door, there is a loud roar from the back of the room.

'A bulls-eye. The bugger, eh!' Dekker's eyes are shining. 'You'll be all right for the moment, won't you? They're a friendly bunch.' With a quick squeeze of her elbow, he edges towards the game.

She stands uncertainly at the margin of the room, smiling too widely, her eyes scanning the crowd. This house is identical to the one she has just come from – she can't yet call it her own – except that here the drinks cupboard has been moved in front of the sliding doors, and the dining table backwards into the lounge area to leave space for the noisy knot of men clustered in front of two dart boards. At the other end of the room, the lights are dimmed and those who aren't playing darts are trying to talk over the music. She had decided to wear a caftan, the one caftan she'd brought with her, only because there it was at the top of her still-packed case and she is relieved to see that although most of the women are wearing long skirts, at least two other women are dressed similarly. A punchbowl stands on a table in a corner of the lounge alongside the record player and she is making her way in that direction when a tall dark man slides in front of her. He holds out his hand.

'Well, I must say, you look jolly lonely, old girl. Erin Richardson, mine host, at your service. You must be Dana. When did you get in? Where's that rat Dekker? Deserted you already, has he? I've have to have a word with him about leaving you alone like this. Now what can I get you to drink. Punch, beer, wine? Can't vouch for the quality of the *sid*, but the wine, of course, is excellent – my wife Vick makes it herself – and there's a lager that's even better brewed by none other than…' He points back at himself, his whole face wreathed in smiles, real smiles. She likes him instantly.

'Sid? What's sid?'

'*Sid*? Short for *sidiki*. Means friend in Arabic. But that stuff can be a somewhat false friend, I'm afraid. It's a clear alcohol, something like gin, made from sugar. Used on camp most of the time as a base for what can be a good punch. Like this one. But go easy. You can't taste the bugger, but it's working away underneath all right. Believe someone who found out the hard way!' He fills a glass with the lemony liquid, floats chunks of orange, pineapple and glacé cherries on top, hands it to her, and turns to a young Korean woman standing with her back to the wall.

'Now let me just introduce you to Cho-hee here and I'll leave you two girls to get to know each other…' He raises his glass and disappears towards the kitchen.

'Cho-hee? That's a pretty name. And unusual…'

The young woman flushes.

'In Korea, not so unusual, see. Many girls have. Meaning beautiful. Also happy. So happy to have this name.'

'Have you been here long?'

'Just arrive. Week before. No. More.' She shakes her head, holds up two fingers. 'Like this.'

'Me, too. Just arrived, I mean.'

'You like?' She peers out from under her straight black fringe.

'Too soon to tell! Between here and the airport is all I've seen so far. I've been here only a few hours. Not much to go on. But the house is good. I'm looking forward to seeing what's outside the compound wall. Something of the place.'

'How long stay? You?'

'Six months. Maybe less. I'm not sure. And you?'

Cho-hee's hesitation mirrors her own.

'Also not sure. My husband. He like very much here. Work, yes, plenty. While back home, not. And…' she rubs her thumb and forefinger together, 'Saving money, also. Make house back home. House first, then baby. Understan'?'

She nods. The salary package that many employees negotiated was tax-free, a tidy sum in any currency and with nothing to spend it on most returned home with the majority intact, a huge incentive, she supposes, for putting one's life on hold for a year or more. The only problem was that it was addictive, Dekker had said. The more you saved, the more you needed to save. Midas gone nuts. She finishes her glass of punch. Erin is right. It tastes like pineapple juice, slips down just as quickly. A small circle gathering about them. The questions repeat.

How long have you been here? How long will you stay? What do you think of Saudi Arabia? Of the camp? Of the tiresome marble floors? Can't wash them with the hard water, you know…they go all smeary as if you've wiped them with milk. Whose wife are you? Over and over. The party moves around her, so in the end she is folding in on herself. She still doesn't feel quite real; it's as if she's a character in one of her own dreams.

She turns to back out of the group to move towards the couch set in a quieter part of the room, but one of the men has peeled himself away from the darts crowd to block the path.

'You're Dekker's wife, aren't you? Thought I'd better introduce myself. David Devenish' He grinned and gestured with his glass. 'I help to keep this crowd in order.'

She holds out her hand. 'Hello. Yes, I'm Dekker's wife. Dana…' She almost says Novotny, catches herself in time. Something she hasn't thought of until now, but Novotny is her professional name, part of an early negotiation with Dekker that her name was not only tied to her sense of who she was, but that it made sense to keep it for professional reasons too. But now? She is not yet ready for Dana Malan. Caught between one name and the next, she's conscious that her given name sounds a little lonely hanging in the air without a patronymic.

Smoothly he steps in to fill the gap.

'If anything goes wrong, day or night, just knock on the door.'

'Oh, I'm sure everything runs like clockwork.' She smiles back at him. His fingers stray to his collar and he takes a sip from his glass.

'I wish! Look, I'd like to say welcome to al-Khasi and get some idea of your first impressions. And to ask if everything's okay with the house? To say also that part of my job description is to offer a short Cook's tour of the area. Have you seen much of the place so far? And if not, fancy a short jaunt to see the sights tomorrow?'

'I've only just got in, haven't yet unpacked…'

'All the same. It's a good way to familiarize yourself with the place and it's all part of the service.' He grins, pushes back a flop of dark hair, drains his glass. 'Well, that's me for bed now. I'll call for you tomorrow morning then. Nine-ish all right?' He slides away and she drops onto the couch.

She is almost asleep when Erin taps the bowl of a glass with the handle of a knife. 'Just wanted to say that here, surrounded as we are by all this sand, it's hard to remember that it's Christmas coming up in only two weeks' time. Back home, or so they write me, it's going to be a white one this year. Snowball fights, skating on the lakes, crystals on the window panes. And plain bloody freezing! So charge your glasses, guys and gals, grab a seat and we'll do a bit of harking back and forth as we listen to a spot of Christmas music!' He selects a record, lets the needle down just as Dekker appears in front of her.

He smiles and drops on the sofa beside her, folds his arm around her shoulders. She settles her head against his chest, snuggles in. Glasses sway.

I'm dreaming of a white Christmas
Just like the ones I used to know

Out of Place

A union of snow and sand. A window-seat on a plane landing in Beirut where sand and snow coalesced at the foot of the mountains. Now here a room full of people out of place, minds and hearts full of snow in the oil-rich desert. Everyone close. Leaning against their men, defenders of the household. White smiles, tight and two-dimensional as a photograph. Except for Cho-hee. Whose face glints in the dimmed light until she places it in the cup of her open hands.

Later that night, undressing for bed, she tells Dekker about the next morning's sightseeing. He laughs.

'Good for Devenish,' he says. 'Make himself useful for a change. You'll get some perspective on the place. And, heh, who knows…if he enjoys himself enough, he might decide to give me that raise he's been holding off on.'

FOUR

When David Devenish had smiled her into his car that morning, her first surprise was that he did not have a driver. Then she had thought he would drive towards the little hamlet they'd passed through on their way from the airport where she could have looked more closely at the basement windows set below the level of the street and where she might scope the one small shop she'd glimpsed the day before. If she were to be driven by a Korean driver with little common language between them, it would be useful to have an English speaker to describe and explain. But, instead, as he guided the car along the tar roads between the houses of the compound and out through the huge double gates, he'd said he was taking her to the *jebel*.

'*Jebel?*' She wondered if she should call him David or be more formal. Or whether it was necessary to call him anything at all.

'Mountain,' he'd replied. 'Arabic for mountain.' He seemed disinclined to say more and she wondered whether he was regretting his spontaneous invitation as much as she was regretting accepting it. She'd found it hard to get out of bed, had dressed again from the top layer of her case. She found herself wondering whether the rather rigid canvasses she'd tucked so carefully at the bottom of her case had survived the rough airline handling, whether her oils had leaked and what she had packed them next to.

She is searching her mind for something to drop into the silence when he stops the car in front of a hill that appears at first not much more than an exaggerated sand dune.

'Here we are,' he says, breaking his silence and smiling tightly for the first time. 'Hop out and we'll take a hike.'

It takes only a few steps for their shoes to fill with sand and following his example she slips hers off. The gradient of the hill might be slight in comparison to the foothills of the Drakensburgs, but the sand slips and slides under her feet so it is not long before she becomes conscious of the heat of the sun, wishes she'd known beforehand about the climb. Or asked. Or brought a hat with her anyway.

Without warning, about a quarter of the way up, he turns to face her.

'This...' He stops to take in a deep breath. 'Phew...warm already.' He runs his hands over his face, turns back to the view and throws his arms out wide. 'This is what I wanted to show you. You can't quite see al-Khasi itself, the township, such as it is. It's hiding just around that bend there. But you probably saw what little there is to see on your way in anyway and this is as good a spot as any to take in the view. Give you a good overall sense of where you are. Gets steeper as you go on so we probably don't need to climb any further. For now, at least.' He takes out a handkerchief, dabs at the sweat gathering on his forehead. 'Make yourself comfortable. Hot today. Very hot, though not as warm as it's going to get. Northern hemisphere, of course, so this is the coolest part of the year.'

She stands with one hand shading her eyes from the eastern sun, aware of his movements as he drops to the ground beside her. He loosens his tie and undoes the top two buttons of his shirt all in one movement as if he's just arrived home after a hard day's work. 'Something to be said for the safari suits your men-folk wear, I must say.'

Gently he pats the sloping sand beside him. 'Come on,' he says to her. 'Sit for a moment. Just relax, for Chrissakes. Enjoy the view.'

He looks quite relaxed himself with the points of his elbows balancing lightly on his knees, his chin on his hands as he perches there on the incline, his hair mussed from the climb and sticking to his forehead. She would just as soon stand as sit, but when he thumps the sand again she crouches down beside him.

And if it is only that this perspective of her new home proves how insignificant they are compared to the relentless stretches of the sand and sea below, then Dekker is right. It does, on a metaphysical plane somehow as well as geographical, show a person's place in the broader scheme of things.

'Something,' she says. 'There's something really rather wonderful in all that down there. It makes me feel very small. And in a way it reminds me of *Ozymandias* and Shelley's "lone and level sands". Do you remember that one? About the ultimate futility of human endeavour. All this building you guys are doing, the ports, smelters and so forth. Do you ever wonder if, in a hundred years' time, they'll still exist? And whether oil then will still be the big deal it is today?'

He frowns slightly before he tilts his head back to laugh. 'Hey, steady on there. Kind of deep for this time of morning, isn't it? Just enjoy the view and the clean air.'

Although the hamlet, the old town, is out of sight, she can make out evenly spaced rows of glinting tin and what she thinks might be the tall concrete wall that circles the compound.

'Isn't that the camp?' She points to the roofs silvering in the sun.

'No. Well, not our compound, that is. That's the Dutch camp. Ours is out of sight, around the side. But over there to the east is the sea of course, the Arabian Gulf. And you can just see a speck…see over there…that's the island of Bahrain. And up there.' He swivels his body to point in the other direction. 'You see way up the coast? Where you can only just make out something happening and a sort of haze above it? That's the American Aramco. Small city, that one, with its own shopping centres, schools, churches. Well worth a look.' He pauses. Pats the sand again. 'What are you doing so far away? Come here.' His hand drops on her thigh so suddenly she flinches. 'What's the matter?' As he reaches for the buttons on her blouse she jerks backwards, loses her balance on the shifting sand. She falls on her back, rolls away from him as he lunges.

It's hot, the sun so bright it steals the colour from the day as it falls across the careless grin on his face. It could just be that he's having a bit of a game. She slaps his hands away, wanting to strike his face, but he's Dekker's boss, he's Dekker's boss, repeats in her brain like a tangle of song. She tries to get to her feet but the sand slides from beneath her. Her breath starts to catch.

'I'm sorry,' she says. 'If I gave you the wrong idea last night. It certainly wasn't…'

'Don't talk,' he mutters. 'Talking only gets in the way. Only gets in the way.' He keeps repeating the phrase like a litany as he struggles with the buttons of her shirt with that fixed grin that belies he has any serious intent, with a look both patient and tolerant, sleepy almost, at odds with the glint of the sun in his irises and the slippery way his hands are darting about. She has the feeling he wants to rip her shirt, but doesn't quite dare. Her first day of a new start…and it has led to this. She twists sideways, rolls twice until she is on her knees.

'I thought you meant what you said. I thought you meant the sights.' She's appealing to the urbane man of the night before. The man who holds one of the top jobs on the site where her husband works and is, so he says, also in charge of the camp and all its people. Which now includes her.

'That was rather naïve of you, wasn't it? Wouldn't you say that was just a touch stupid?'

What are your first impressions? That had been his first question. How was she getting on? Did she have everything she needed in the house? Did it fulfill her expectations? How much had she seen of the village? How long was she expecting to stay in al-Khasi? Cho-hee, the group of women, their questions, his questions. Voices merge as she faces him, still on her knees in the sand.

His eyes are hard and bright as he grabs at her. But she is quicker, on her feet now, and she manages to keep her balance as she staggers back. They are both sticky with sand and sweat and she has the horrible feeling that it is the struggle in all this that he's enjoying as much as anything.

'Not only me. It wasn't only me who thought you meant sightseeing,' she says, her breath hot in her throat. 'It was Dekker as well. In fact we both thought it very generous of you to offer to take the time to show me around.'

'Dekker? Dekker Malan?' He looks at her as if she's said something rather clever and amazing. Like, look, there's a black cloud lurking on the horizon. Or, isn't that an iceberg being towed up the Gulf? He struggles onto his bottom, sits for a moment facing forward, struggling to regulate his breathing as his face dapples, tight white blotches appearing from under the red. 'Dekker? You told your husband? You mean…your husband knows you're here?'

'He knows that I'm with you. Yes, of course. Naturally I told Dekker.'

There is a bulge in his throat. A snake with a frog in its gullet that won't go up or down. She pushes down an urge to giggle, wonders whether she is on the edge of hysteria as she tugs her clothes around, her fingers clumsy and swollen with the heat. She feels as if she's spent a hot day at the beach. A world of grit. As he turns from her to adjust his trousers, suddenly private with all he had wanted to make public, she realizes that by lucky chance she had stumbled on perhaps the only remark that would have stopped him. Tentatively, she turns her back on him and begins to make her way down the hill, wondering if she'll be able to outrun him if he tries to catch her, knows she doesn't have a chance.

The sand melts against her bare soles, sharp stinging needles, hot as molten glass.

FIVE

She likes to watch him shave, has missed it even; her eyes follow the sweep of his hand as the razor slicks a path through the mass of meringue. In the early days, they liked to kiss through the mess of foam and she smiles to remember how she'd laughed at the bubbles bursting against her skin… She sits on the edge of the bath watching his eyes watch hers from the mirror as he angles his chin towards the blade.

'So, what are you going to do today?'

Today, this second day. She swallows. Tries to consign the day before to the past, wipe from her mind the way Devenish's eyes had latched onto hers, the way her soles still stung from the hot sand, the way Dekker had turned from her when she told him.

'I'd like to settle straight into it.'

'Straight into it? Into what exactly?'

'Painting. Into my painting. Remember? I wrote you about it? About the series I was planning. I thought instead of a journal that I'd…'

'But you're barely unpacked.' He swishes the razor rapidly through the water. 'What's the hurry, eh?' His eyes, darker now, still watching hers, his head framed in the silver glassiness of the mirror and his throat tight as his fingers probe his skin, searching out the rough. 'Take time to familiarize yourself with the place. It's a golden opportunity. Besides I thought you loathed painting.'

'Well, yes, I do. Did. But I wrote you about how breaking through that…well, that block I have…might be a useful way to spend my time here. Perhaps now I'm out from the folks, from my father, I might find it easier. You see, I thought I'd work in the mornings. Keep the afternoons for sightseeing. And yes, unpack first, you're right. But there's not much to unpack. A couple of cases…'

'And the rest of your stuff? The boxes I brought over with me. In any case, I didn't mean unpacked in the *literal* sense.' He swished the blade impatiently through the water. 'I was thinking more broadly. Like relax, Dana for once. But not relax into more work. Relax into enjoyment. Read a book. Meet one of the ladies from the other night for a cup of coffee; sleep, sunbathe, go for a drive. What is it about you that you have to be so rigid?' His tone has tightened.

I was taken for a drive yesterday, she thinks. Her hands grip the edge of the bath. Not so soon. Not so soon after the warm time in bed. She brushes a grain of sand from the edge of the bath.

'It's not that. Just that if I don't force myself into some sort of routine from the start I'm lost…'

'Force. Routine. Lost.' He drops the razor into the basin, reaches for a towel. 'Work. Work. Work. Can't you stop driving yourself for long enough to get over jet lag even?' His eyes – almost navy now – blaze briefly before his face disappears into the towel.

She takes a deep breath. 'All right. I'd forgotten already. Take it easy. I know.'

'Good.' His smile is back. He drops the towel over the rail. 'Good girl. The sooner you make friends, the happier you'll be. And you can't do that by osmosis. You have to put a little effort into it. Or if you like, I can send the car back for you in an hour or so? There's a market not far from the village that'll interest you. Take the camera. Top drawer in the bedroom. Click, click, eh?'

She smiles back at him, minutes later he is dressed and gone. The door slams with a sound-feel of small shocks. She hears him greet the driver, the oiled grunt of the car door closing. She sits quite still until the sound of him no longer vibrates through her body. And then it's so quiet she can hear her own breath. And then her own words. It's imperative that I work while I'm there. Imperative. At least two paintings…or the start of a series of drawings perhaps…two good works must result from this time. I promise myself…I promise.

Her father was that rare being – someone who had managed to make a living, and quite a decent living, as an artist. That she would not only follow his example in her choice of profession, but also be as successful as he, was not just an expectation, but a family given. From there, it was a short step to the day she found herself at art school standing in front of an easel, drawing perspective in the shape of streets and buildings that were supposed to shrink progressively into a dot that signified distance. She stuck at it for two terms before she dropped out. It was not a humiliating three months; it was not that she disliked what she was doing or that her grades were bad or that she made any waves at all. And that was just it. It was a period in which she hardly knew she was alive, a period of what her grandmother would have termed 'glorious mediocrity'. The only difficulty in withdrawing from the course came in the disappointment she caused her father, made even more acute when she took a job as typist for a firm of accountants. Two years later, she answered an advertisement for a secretarial job in the cataloguing department of the Wits museum. She passed the first interview and was one of two on the shortlist.

'I do so hope I get it,' she'd said to the anonymous voice the other end, gripping the receiver so hard that her hand ached when she hung up. And then the emptiness that followed a few days later when she found she hadn't been chosen. 'But there's something else you may be interested in,' he'd continued on the occasion of this second conversation. 'Another possibility has cropped up that may suit you even better. How would you like a job cataloguing?' She'd gasped, a sharp indrawn breath as if she'd just remembered she should be somewhere else.

She was ecstatic, her parents less so. 'Cataloguing in a museum? Making lists? You? A dusty dead-end job like that. You'll end up as dry as one of your fossils,' her father had grumbled. 'A gallery, an art gallery. Yes, that I could understand. But museums? Places stink of dust and decay. All those empty eye sockets and rattling bones in their dirty glass coffins.' He had looked at her as if he had trouble believing her to be his daughter. 'You didn't give it long enough, you know. You gave up too easily. It surprises me. I must say.' He turned away, shaking his head.

Although she knew he was referring to art school, his words had returned her to an earlier time and the blast of shame she'd felt as a child proudly showing him her painting of a group of her young friends. There were three girls in the picture and they were dancing carelessly under a bold yellow sun. Their lips were redder than the Wicked Queen's apple and their dresses were as white as her Sunday best. When her art teacher pointed out that the white dresses failed against the white of the paper, she had solved the problem by outlining the figures and their clothes in blue to match the sky. When her painting had been chosen as one of the top three in her class for that term and stuck up on the wall for all to see, she was in a fever all that week for it to be taken down so she could take it home to show her father.

She was smiling more broadly than the young girls in her picture when she handed it to him, pointing out the thumb-tack holes in the corners as proof that it had been hung before standing, breathless, with her hands clasped behind her back. So she was unprepared for Peter Novotny's burst of laughter. He was not an unkind man, but in her memories of that moment he is not kind.

'But these are bities,' he told her, handing the drawing back to her. 'You've drawn bities.'

Bities? What were *bities*? She could only think he was referring to the way she had delineated the figures. To the way she had contained the girls. She tried them again in coloured dresses, in bright reds and soft yellows, but she never again captured the abandoned way they had danced in the sunlight. It was almost as if they owed their freedom to their blue outlines. Almost as if they had to do it their way, as strange as it was.

'Why don't you try still life instead?' he'd said one day. 'It's not really a matter of having talent or not having talent, you know. It's a question of technique. Craft. Perspective. These things can be learned. But it's mainly practice. Practice is all it is.'

So she had tried harder. And many years after that, in the old art school building, not wanting to give up, she'd worked harder still. But the watercolours wept on the page, the oils smelled rank and clumped together, her brush was wood to the tip. On the other hand, with the secretarial job had come a pleasing predictability. She knew what she had to do and when and why she had to do it. And it came with a pay packet, a small brown envelope she collected every week, and which gradually became fatter along with the little shifts upwards in terms of responsibility. When the museum job was offered, she knew she was ready. Three weeks after the phone call, she was learning her new job, two years after that she was assistant archivist, and then there was a short stint in displays in readiness for a sponsored tour of the world's most significant museums. She had headed up the archival department for the last four years and again, recently, there had been some talk of being in line for another promotion.

She's still perched on the edge of the bathtub when she hears a knock at the door. The driver back already? Surely she hasn't sat and dreamed for so long. She glances at her watch. For an instant, it's an intrusion she doesn't want; a split-second later she rushes to pull on jeans, a blouse, sandals.

'Coming. Just a tick.'

She races at the door, pauses with her hand on the knob and takes a breath before she opens it, quite sedately then, to a woman piggy-backing a little boy and dressed in a yellow caftan with huge sleeves like Mandarin's robe. The woman grins and slips into a bow so deep that her long pony-tail flips over her head to sweep the sand at their feet and the child's fingers dig into his mother's shoulders. He screams with the fun of it.

'Hello. I'm Poppy,' she says. 'Is it much, much too early in the day or can I come in?'

SIX

'I promised Dekker I'd drop in on you. Sorry for the lack of any sort of notice. If it had been way back when, your butler would have answered the door and I would have left a calling card. But with no telephones yet. Though they tell us we'll have them one day. And then just imagine the luxury of not having to drive fifty miles to wait in line at the post office for an hour to talk to the chaps at home for three minutes – that is if you're lucky enough that the connection hangs in that long.

'I'm Poppy,' she says again. 'Laurie's wife.' She pauses, makes a face. 'Makes me sound a bit like an arm or a leg, doesn't it?' She shrugs. 'This red-haired ruffian on my back is, quite naturally, Rufus. And I have Rachel in the pouch.' She pats her belly. 'At least, I hope and pray most sincerely it's a Rachel. Outnumbered two to one by the male sex in our household at present.'

'Hello. All of you. I'm Dana.' She hesitates. 'The house, I'm afraid…'

'All our houses. Always. Impossible for them to live up to our expectations. Or us to theirs. Don't worry about it. Don't even think of it.' Poppy rustles in, swings the child down. 'Down you, too heavy. Behave yourself until the big hand of that clock over there gets to the six and then you can have a half-biccy.' She upends a small sack of toys onto the carpet, throws herself on the couch and adjusts the scrap of chiffon at her neck all in one flowing movement that for an uncomfortable moment reminds Dana of David Devenish. 'Phew, hanging out for the second trimester. A lot easier than the first and beats the shit out of the third. I'll be glad when this breeding business is all over, I can tell you.

'But this is a good place to have them. Gives you something to worry about. Just to put me in some sort of context: Somewhat by default – and I suspect only because I'm one of the longest female residents on this camp – I've been dubbed the unofficial organizer here.' She screws up her nose. 'Everything from tennis matches, bus to al-Dhuraf, welcoming committee of one. Anything and everything but bridge. Can't stand the game. And these days I tend to stay away from the eternal parties – there's one just about every night somewhere on the camp.

'What about you? No children obviously? What are you going to do while you're here? Plans? Dreams? Desires?' She leans forward. 'Tell all to Aunt Poppy.' She makes a face again.

Dana smiles back at her. 'Well, I'm here. Just. With all the time in the world to enjoy myself. But plans, dreams, desires?' She shrugs. 'Not sure. Sort of on hold for the moment. Meanwhile, what would you like to drink? Would you like a cup of tea? Coffee?'

'What a relief not to be offered wine! Tea, please, strong as you like, lots of milk, oodles of sugar. Got to get my jollies somehow. Enjoy?' She turns the word over in her mouth. '*Enjoy.* Yes, that's so. Have you got out much yet?'

'Just...' Dana pauses, halfway out of the room, wondering just how much to tell. In the end the words take over. 'Today – quite shortly – I'm meant to be going to the markets. I think. And yesterday, my first day, Dekker's boss took me...sightseeing. So far, that's it.'

'The *jebel*, quite naturally.' Poppy's lips twist. She looks down suddenly, puts her hand out to straighten the little boy's t'shirt. 'Up to his old tricks, is he?'

'His old tricks? Meaning?'

'Meaning...oh, later.' She waves her hand and her grin is back. 'Tell me first about you. I'm hungry for news about the real world. Where do you come from and where are you going pretty maid? Did you work? How long are you going to be here?'

'Okay, okay. Come with me while I make the tea. In a nutshell? My life condensed into ten seconds: I'm half-Australian, half-German, born in Sydney, spent almost all my life in Jo'burg. Briefly at art school. Then worked in a museum. Loved it...' She stops.

'And you met hubby – obviously not at art school? Or the museum?'

'Well no, actually. We met at a red light...'

'Red light? Hmm...what sort of red light? Accident? Or maybe some sort of district you worked in.' Poppy rolls her eyes and cocks an eyebrow.

Dana chuckles. 'Not exactly! It was by design on his part. Or maybe all part of the grander design. Both of us waiting for the traffic lights to change.' She smiles over her shoulder as she takes the milk from the fridge. 'He's a marine expert – among other things. His work is very methodical and studied whereas, well, mine is balanced between the archaic and the glorious uncertainties of creative impulse. Anyway, by the time we'd figured out that we didn't have too much in common, we'd fallen for each other on the basis, I suppose, that opposites attract. We married four years ago.'

'What job did you have?'

'Did? I suppose it is *did* now. I keep forgetting…' There is a catch in the lightness of her quick laugh. 'Hard to swallow, I have to say. Just yet anyway. My work – what I was doing before I came here until as recently as last Thursday in fact – was archivist for the Wits Museum on the edge of the city, the city of Johannesburg that is. Great job, great mix of work and people. I started there about six years ago, bit more, with the ordinary stuff like cataloguing and keeping records, went on to the setting up of installations, interpretation of artefacts.' Eyes shining, she leans her elbows on the counter.

'Interpretation, you see, representation…that sort of stuff is just moving into a new phase in Europe and the United States. The new ethnology. There was – still is – a lot of opposition to that in South Africa, of course. I was in the middle of setting up a new display, an exhibit of artifacts of one of the South African tribes – the Matabele – and it was halted mid-stride because…' She stops. 'Oops, I got carried away. Boring. Boring. And we've forgotten your little boy. Let's go back into the other room.'

'Fascinating. Not boring,' says Poppy when they are settled back in the lounge where Rufus' eyes haven't moved from the minute-hand. She takes a cautious sip of the hot sweet tea, places the cup carefully in the centre of the coffee table and looks straight into Dana's eyes. 'When bi-national girl meets her man, she ditches fascinating job in Johannesburg for life on an English camp on the fringe of the Arabian desert. I'm tempted to say that I wish you the best of British luck, but it has a somewhat ironic after-life attached, that saying.'

'And you, Poppy?'

'Me? Nothing so exotic, I'm afraid. Secretary to a lawyer in the other life. Kidded myself I was sort of paralegal, but I didn't have the critical bits of paper. Only aptitude. Yes, attitude and aptitude. Anyway, loved it to bits. More than that. Otherwise English back to William the Conqueror. Now – in my current iteration – I'm a breeder. Nothing else to tell except, as I said, I'm the one they usually send to greet newcomers to the site. Been here three years, almost from the beginning. Laurence – Laurie – is more interesting. He's been in these parts forever. You'll love him.' She pauses to pick up her cup again. 'And so – how do you plan to pass the time joyfully? More...' she coughs and looks sideways at Dana. 'More sights?'

Yesterday is still too close to discuss and for a moment Poppy is distracted by giving Rufus his half-hour reward.

'Certainly no more sights from the side of the hill. I sincerely hope. But apparently, well, I'm sure there's heaps to see here. And I'm anxious, you see, to do the right thing. Culturally, that is. Anything you can tell me.'

'Yes, heaps. Heaps to do, that is. Well, on the one hand there is and on the other there isn't. You've got to get outside the wall, you…'

'I've got a driver. Apparently that helps.'

'It's not that sort of wall I'm talking about. Let's see. How can I best put this? From the cultural angle you mentioned, the first thing to understand about this country is that it's a privilege for you to be here. Not, perhaps, from your point of view, but from everyone else's…'

'Yes, Dekker said.'

'And he's right. In order not to abuse that privilege, you have to cover up when you go out. From chin to foot and your arms. To the wrists, to be more exact. But I'm sure Dekker's got you up to speed on all this? I've known the religious police – the *mutaween* – to tap women on whatever part of their bodies that are showing – throat, wrists, legs, breasts – with their canes up in al-Dhuraf. And photographs. Be careful how and when you use a camera. Some of them, the Arabs that is, are sensitive about having their photo taken. I don't know whether it's a religious thing or whether it's part of a deeper core belief system. Something like stealing the soul. Or could just be a mistrust of having something poked in their faces. It is a bit cheeky when you come to think about it. Just snapping people without a by-your-leave.' She stops, her head on one side, listening. 'Just a minute. I think I heard something?' The knock comes again. 'Someone at the front door?'

'Completely forgot. The driver. I'm supposed to go out. Damn. Forgot all about it…' She goes to rise, but Poppy places a hand on her arm.

'Do I detect reluctance?'

She shakes her head. 'Not really. It's only that I want to sort of stabilize myself for a few days, get properly unpacked and organized. But I also have this niggling feeling that I should get out.'

'Why?'

'Because. Because, oh well, I don't want to rock the boat. The driver'll tell Dekker and...'

Poppy raises her hand.

'Just a sec. May I talk to him?' She takes her tea with her as she goes to the door, greets the driver with a smile in her voice. 'Madam is not well. Please do not worry about it today.' She closes the door gently, turns her smile back to Dana. 'There. It's that easy.'

Dana looks down at the child's chocolate fingers on the cream of the leather couch and then at her own feet which rest neatly side by side, almost touching each other.

'But it's a lie,' she says.

'Yes, it is. It's an outright lie to stop you being resentful later. Because once you've gone to the *suq*, been down the coast to get fresh prawns and up to al-Dhuraf to buy a caftan and then another and another, you'll have done all the sights you'll be able to do without your husband as escort. I agree: it's an utter lie. But a harmless one, too. To keep your sanity.'

'But a hundred years ago, Jane Digby...'

'I don't know about a Jane Digby. And I wasn't around a hundred years ago. Although it sometimes feels like it. All I know is here and how to survive the current day. In the climate of this compound.' Poppy pauses. 'But I know, too, that another name for a white lie is prevarication. I used to deal with a lot of prevarication at the law office. The dictionary says something like it's a timely deflection of the truth with the aim of stopping someone getting hurt. In this case, two people. Less harm, that way. And the Korean driver gets time off to return to his cabin to start off another batch of *kimchee*.'

'*Kimchee?*'

'Pickled cabbage. If you can get past the awful smell, it actually tastes rather good.' She stoops to gather up the toys. 'Now I'm going to take my interfering self away and let you have the space you crave. Before too long it'll be time to get lunch for the men anyway. And then,' she rolls her eyes again, 'there's the dreaded siesta when they suddenly come alive.'

Poppy pauses at the door.

'Only one more thing. I think the only thing that differentiates one person from another – as humans that is – is our dreams. You have to follow them through. As for rocking the boat – the sad thing about boats is if you do nothing, that is, don't stick up for yourself, if one person does all the work, makes all the decisions, the boat is already unbalanced, isn't it?

'Lovely that you're going to be here. Oh, and in terms of cultural, just one more thing. You don't have to wear the *chador* or *burqa* or whatever you want to call it – to drape yourself from head to toe like a black ghost – the local women do, but not us. Not yet anyway. And you can almost wear what you like within the compound. Although…' She wriggles her shoulders. 'To tell the truth, it begins to feel slightly weird after a while, wearing less rather than more. The maintenance men, you see, they're always about.'

She drops her long pony-tail down towards Rufus. 'All right, you've been a great kid, Ruf. Time now to make lunch for Daddy. Grab my hair, get ready to swing up. One, two…' As she steps onto the sand, she turns back. 'Oh, and yes, I've been asked to tell you. There's a party at the Wilsons' tomorrow night. Dekker'll fill you in. Cheers.'

Dana watches until the figure with the hump on her back disappears between the houses and the only thing left is her tracks in the sand. What reason should she give Dekker for sending the driver away? That it was as simple as a headache? Trite, but as Poppy said, no harm.

But as it was, he forgot to ask her. Both that lunchtime and on his return home at the end of the day. By which time she was so relieved that she didn't have to lie, she decided that the events of the morning, like those of the day before, were better consigned to the past.

That was the beginning.

But by the next morning he has remembered.

'My goodness, is that the time already,' he says pulling away from her and swinging his feet off the bed. 'Time I was away. No, don't get up. Leisurely. Remember, leisure. Which reminds me. I didn't ask you about yesterday's jaunt. Did you get out?'

'No. No, I didn't. I felt a bit – off.' Surprising how easily the words slipped off her tongue as if they were gathered waiting at the tip.

He knots the belt of his bathrobe, gives it an extra tug. 'Well you can do it today, then?'

'Yes, yes. Perhaps if you wouldn't mind sending him anyway, I'll see how the morning pans out.'

'Good girl. I knew you'd get right into it.' He bends to kiss her. 'And something else.' He sits again on the edge of the bed. 'Look. I'm sorry about the other morning. I apologise if I sounded a bit sharp. It's just that…aah.' He sighs. 'Hey, Dana, I do wish you would begin to act like a married woman.'

'That stupid sightseeing thing.' She swings her own legs off the bed, clasps her hands between her knees. 'I said I'm sorry. I *am* sorry. I had absolutely no idea it would turn out like that…'

'Not that,' he breaks in, waving his hand. 'Not that at all. That's nothing.' To her surprise, he chuckles. 'I meant to tell you. The day after that. Just yesterday. It was really very funny. I stood in the corridor – they're narrow, you know, the corridors in the site trailer – as Devenish was coming towards me. And he looked extremely, well, you could say anxious. Passed me side on, almost flattened to the side of the wall. A smile on his face, a very nervous smile. No.' He rubs his hands tightly together, flicks one against the other. 'No, I think you'll find that's all finished. He's unlikely to try that sort of stunt again. Meanwhile, let's just say that he's in my debt, shall we, and leave it there?' She's about to speak, but he raises his hand.

'If you would just let me finish, Dana please. I meant I'm sorry for being annoyed yesterday morning. It's just that I don't want you to feel you have to do anything at all while you are here. You don't have to work, to pretend to be busy, none of that. No daily drudge.'

But it wasn't a drudge, she wants to say. Work was never a drudge. Quite the opposite in fact. When I turned the car onto the motorway and there was the ugliest city in the world waiting for me, I wasn't thinking drudge, I wasn't even thinking career although you'll never believe me however often I tell you. The truth is that I was merely thinking of the day ahead. Of being part of something, of a team, of having people around, of feeling that my opinion mattered, of sharing in decisions, of doing something that outlasted the day I did it in. And always there would be another strata of thought that underlay the decisions I knew I'd have to make that day or that week about the projects waiting for my attention. Things like, how best to tell the story of the jade figurine. Or the broken set of spears.

'There'll be so much to do here. So much to do. Just you see. Some of the wives even make their own wine. You can take your camera. Go off to the town. Lots of parties. A party almost every night. You'll see. You won't want to leave. You won't want to leave.'

This endless battle we have, she thinks. He's not hearing me. Through the wetness that arrives quite unexpectedly on her lashes she sees him moving towards her, the skin either side of his eyes crinkling, his fingers tugging loose the knot of his robe.

'Besides I didn't marry you to have you work. I married you because I wanted a wife. Don't you see?'

But what she doesn't know is that in the end he will be right and she will find it difficult to leave. All she can think when he's finally gone that morning and she's still in bed is that she still hasn't told him about Poppy's visit. About her arriving at the door with the child clinging to her back.

SEVEN

Tucked among her shoes at the bottom of the second case are brushes, pencils, crayons and a small pack of oils in the thin tin tubes which she finds she had wrapped carefully in plastic after all. Pressed flat into the base of the first case are her canvases and a sketching pad. Bring everything you might need, Dekker had urged. You won't be able to get anything out of the ordinary here. One of the boards has a bash on one corner – repacked too hastily in front of the Arab customs official with the wisp of beard and the shiny black Malacca cane – but otherwise they are creamy white and rather terrifying ready.

A clean start. The thought arrives with the hint of an echo about it – and it surprises her. She is unsure whether it means that the past, in comparison, is besmirched in some way, sullied somehow compared to what might be ahead?

And if so, does that relate to the past days or years or the whole of her life until now? The questions hover, puncturing her energy. She sits on the bed with one of the boards in her hands, runs her hand over the weave of the surface, wonders where she can prop it up. Time without appointments, meetings, deadlines and decisions is an open-ended thing: a dragon with its teeth, fiery breath and scales removed, so it's more like a gecko waiting on a bare-faced wall for day to turn to night, for the food source to proliferate, for a mosquito to make a mistake.

The gloom in the bedroom tightens; she thinks for a moment of flinging herself back on the bed. She needs a plan, even enjoyment takes planning. Perhaps she should start the day again? She glances at her watch where the second hand moves grudgingly around the dial; absently, she winds it. It's still on Johannesburg time and she is reluctant to re-set it, finds a sense of connection in this self-deception, some consolation in the knowledge that the world back there is still fast asleep, that she is not sitting on the edge of a bed in a dark room while they are letting themselves into their offices or opening up the halls, turning on the installations, flicking the switches one by one, converging for chatter at the coffee machine. She fights again the urge to lie down, is surprised at the effort it takes to get up and walk into the lounge.

Clearly the only place practical to set up her work is somewhere in this rectangle of lounge and dining room. Placing the canvas on the dining table she moves towards the wall of glass, sliding one half of the door open onto what could be a patio, but isn't. She steps down into the sand, the first time she has been out of this side of the house, nothing but loose sand between here and the back steps of the neighbours in front, the gaps in between leading to yet another row of houses. No boundary between one home and the next, no demarcation of territory between families: the only limits here are those that divide the compound itself from the country it's set in. She bends to scoop up a handful of sand, opens her fingers so it runs out, every last grain of it. Slowly she raises the heel of her foot to step up backwards into the house, slides the door closed.

It's different, Dana. It's just because it's different. Time. Takes time to adjust. Taking a deep breath, she turns from the glass, picks up the board and leans it against the back of a chair, stands back, head on one side. With the light flooding in behind her, the canvas glows, this time of the day at least. She'll need an easel of course, but in this Dekker has reassured her.

'Easy enough to get something that size knocked together on site what with all the maintenance men wandering back and forth looking for something to do.' She'll have to remind him. Or maybe it is up to her to ask one of the guys. What had Poppy said? 'If something goes wrong – light bulb, washing machine or anything really – just stick your head out the door and collar one of those guys in yellow overalls.'

But meanwhile, she thinks, this is as good a place as any to start.

I don't want it just to be good, she says to the room. *I want it to be much much more than that. I want to allow the painting to create itself, to speak to itself, so that on one level it's alive. And if that all sounds too gloriously egotistical, so what?*

But it's then – as she sits in the sunlight gazing at the white board and its possibilities – that the three bities start to dance across the canvas. The small shock at the sight of the three white-clothed figures in their blue outlines and then her father's face. The tug of guilt that reminds her that this is the first time since she arrived she's thought of her parents. *I must write, tell them I've arrived safely* – it'll be weeks before they get the letter. And why had she never asked her father exactly what he meant by bities? Now, she supposes, he will not be able to remember something that to him must have been a throwaway line, a spontaneous reaction to his only child's lack of talent. Originally the thick blue outlines were to serve a purpose, to make the figures stand out from the paper. Later that was the only way she could get them to dance, to be really free. She's puzzling the contradiction of caged figures and freedom when the knock startles her.

She shakes herself back to the moment. Not again. A trip out. Not really convenient right now. Her eyes flick back to the canvas. But on the other hand, why not? She has avoided it for a week and she's here for the experiences of Arabia after all. She needs that to be able to paint, to draw. She needs to feed her imagination. She needs to get out, to replace the memory of the last drive with another.

She moves to the door, remembers Poppy's injunction.

'Half an hour, please,' she says to the driver. 'Would you mind coming back in half an hour?' She will make sandwiches for lunch and make sure she is back before noon.

One step at a time. She speaks aloud as she stands on tiptoe to place the board on top of the dining room dresser.

The trip to the markets is bland and smooth. So seamlessly is she driven between one place and another that when she steps out of the car she feels like a time traveller set down in an ancient land. Standing awkwardly on a broken stretch of pavement, she is separated from the *suq* across the road by the rows of silvery fish drying on the length of hessian that follows the contour of the street. Not quite decaying, she thinks as she steps over them, but decidedly sniffy and then smiles to think this is a term her father would use. After that, she ceases to think separate thoughts. The market closes around her. The burn of the sun releases a powerful frisson of zest from the platters of spices in their heaping browns and golds and yellows. Two Arabs slump over tiny cups of sticky black coffee that sit on the sloping table between them, their eyelids heavy as they suck at their hubble-bubble pipes. Further along, the vibrant colours of a stall selling material, the bolts of brightly coloured cloth arraigned on shelves like rows of massive books. It's a wonder they don't fade, she thinks, these silks and satins and brocades, some watered, some encrusted with beading or pearls, others embroidered. And who buys? Surely not the black-clad women about her? Except for their wedding day, perhaps. Feast days? Trips abroad?

She fights the urge to stare, wonders how she can bear not to absorb these impressions, wonders, too, why Poppy was so dismissive of the experience. Perhaps this is something you get used to? Perhaps when you live here and you have ready access to so much difference, it becomes part of the everyday? She has given herself an hour, realizes this is barely enough time to do more than stroll slowly past the stalls that cling to the outer edge of the market. The locals ignore her: the men in their white robes and red-checked headdresses outside the coffee houses and the women in heavy black with baskets over their arms and small children at their sides who hide their heads in their mothers' coarse cloaks as she passes.

She steps to one side as a woman stops in front of her, motions to a sack of rice, raises three fingers. The shopkeeper does not look up as he weighs out the rice. He adds and subtracts a grain here and there, pours the rest into a brown paper bag, drags forth an abacus from a small drawer, flicks at the counters, stretches out his hand. From somewhere among the folds of her robe, the woman brings forth a small bundle of riyals, counts each off separately before handing them to the merchant who pushes them to the back of the drawer. This transaction, like others around her, is conducted in silence. It is, she thinks, like a silent movie, a Charlie Chaplin film, but slower, much slower.

At intervals, the market retreats from the street into alley ways that disappear into blackness; neat stacks of green and gold tins of treacle stand at the entrance of one these passages – at the stall opposite, bundles of knives, forks, spoons, sieves and saucepans hang from hooks and rafters. She would like to spend a morning just wandering. Or a day. Or each day for as long as she likes.

The car is waiting when she turns to leave and it is only as she negotiates the row of drying fish that she remembers she didn't consider whether Dekker needed it to get home. She doesn't even know how far the site office is from the house. Since the Korean driver speaks no English and she no Korean he only looks confused when she tries to ask him how Dekker is getting home for lunch. Easier just to get in the car.

The front door is open and as she rushes in she hears laughter which halts her slightly so she walks more slowly across the lounge to the kitchen. Her husband is at the counter buttering bread. Sitting at the kitchen table taking a large bite out of one of the sandwiches she had assembled earlier is a man she hasn't yet met. Both men turn as she comes in and something shifts so that the sum of three is suddenly less than two.

'Well, isn't someone going to introduce me?' Her words sound heavy. Hang for just an instant in the air between them. And then Dekker gestures with the knife.

'This is Taylor. Kind enough to give me a lift back. Taylor, as you've gathered, this is my wife Dana.'

When, once, a friend had mentioned that she had taken an instant dislike to someone, Dana had asked, 'How on earth can you dislike someone you don't even know?' 'Animals,' said the woman, shrugging. 'At base we're all animals. As humans, we've done a good job of suppressing it, but despite us, there's still a vestige of instinct, sixth sense – or wariness sometimes – that remains.' And now, quite suddenly, Dana understands. Because there is something in the bareness of the smile he gives her that contrasts coldly with the cradle of camaraderie that had existed before her entrance. Something in the crinkling of the skin around his eyes that leaves his eyes untouched. Something in the straightness of his gaze as he hunkers over the bread in his hand, in both hands, not exactly calculating, but not giving anything away either as he looks her over with as objective an assessment as she herself would have given to the claim of a piece of ancient pottery.

Returning his smile briefly, she turns to Dekker. 'Sorry about not being here. Took longer than I thought…'

'Women and shopping.' The laughter spreads in a series of chuckles from one to the other and back again.

'Get some good shots?' Dekker asks.

'Well, no, I didn't take the camera in the end. And I didn't shop. Not exactly. Not shopping exactly.' She spreads her hands as they gaze at her. 'But it was interesting, I have to say. What little I saw of the sook.'

'*Suq*,' Taylor corrects. He pushes his empty plate across the table, gets to his feet. 'Well, I've leave you two to your lunch.' He half-turns towards her, his lips compressed in what might have been a smile. 'I was just asking Dekker here whether you might be interested in a spot of bridge? There's four of us get together Tuesd'ys. My regular partner is away for two, three weeks. Wonderin' whether you'd fill in.' He doesn't like asking she thinks. Bites off his sentences in the same way he dispatched the sandwich.

She pulls out a chair just as Dekker places another plate of sandwiches on the table.

'Oh no. I don't think so. I haven't played for years. And it's never been…'

'You won't need to worry. Average players, all of us. Tuesd'y night then. Pick you up around 6.30.'

'Oh no, not at night. Definitely not in the evening. Dekker…' she appeals.

'Go,' says her husband, turning back to the bread board. 'Go on. Not much else to do here in the evenings. You'll enjoy yourself.'

At the door, Taylor looks back over his shoulder.

'See you 6.30 then. Oh…and thanks for the snack.'

EIGHT

Some days later, she is the first to arrive at Poppy's coffee party, to enter yet another house that is the exact replica of her own, except the leather lounge suite here is brown instead of cream.

Poppy is crouching in the middle of the marble floor picking up small square wooden blocks. She is dressed even more becomingly today in a tan skirt with a loose white blouse, but her face looks tighter and more constrained than when they first met. Perhaps it's the preparation and the clearing-up of toys before the onslaught of visitors. Or perhaps it's her stance, Dana thinks, perched as she is on all fours, backed slightly onto her haunches. For an instant, she is reminded of an animal in a cage.

'A, B, X,' says Poppy carefully. Running her fingers over the raised letters, she drops the blocks into a battered cardboard box. 'Three sides and a flap. It's the fancy stage for our Punch and Judy shows,' she explains, snapping herself into another mood as if she has read Dana's mind. 'Doubles as a temporary toy box in between.' She smiles in a distant sort of way and they laugh. But their laughter stops too sharply and simultaneously; as if quite suddenly they have realized that if they start they may not be able to stop, as if somehow they have asked themselves, 'just what, exactly, is funny?' But then Poppy grins and the grin is different from the smile. It presses right through to her centre and shines out through her eyes. Dana drops to her knees to help her and as she does so something quite solid and real passes from one to the other. It's neither a look, nor a word, and it's not a touch. Something indefinable, Dana thinks, but in that moment she feels like kid in kindy invited to join the group.

'Dekker wants me to go up to al-Dhuraf,' she says. 'Can you come? Tomorrow?'

Poppy hesitates. 'I'd love to, but I can't. Not tomorrow. But next time. Ask me next time.'

It wasn't bad, that coffee morning, she decided afterwards. Apart from the tea-wine, offered as an alternative to coffee and which she wished she had refused, it was rather as she'd imagined an AA meeting, this group of disparate people sitting in a circle, bound together by a set of circumstances. Each anxious to speak their truth, but to do so without giving too much away. Did they all feel as she did: both included and yet excluded from each other's lives? Close. But not snug. A tenuous circle of energy that connected only when there was a splutter. Or a charge.

Tuesday and bridge came around much faster than she would have believed possible. She'd managed to put it out of her mind over the last few days, but now she spends the afternoon trying to remember what she can of her short association with the game.

The day is falling away with the setting sun when Taylor picks her up and it's nearly dark by the time they get to the Dutch camp. And cold. She pulls her cardigan tight around her, wishes she'd worn something warmer.

'S'pose it's summer where you come from.' He closes his door and rubs at the stubble on his chin as his gaze meets hers over the car roof. She can barely see him in the half-light, but she senses his eyes narrowing. His voice thickens. 'Do I drive you into the desert now,' he says. 'Or later.'

Barely able to believe what she hears, she stares, snaps back, her voice even to her own ears sounding clipped and high. 'That's hardly cricket,' she says. Something more than the cool air chills her. She draws herself in.

'It wasn't cricket I was thinkin' of,' he mutters. 'Come on then. They'll be waiting for us and it'll be warmer inside. It can get cold here at night.' He squints upwards as he moves around the car to take her elbow. 'It's the clear sky. Once the sun drops, there's not much to hold in the heat. The name's Tay to my close friends. By the way. You'll find I respond better to that.'

She glares at him: an outline of a man with dark curling hair and sideburns. Dressed in a t'shirt and shorts. Deliberately scruffy.

NINE

The only difficulty about the two-hour trip to al-Dhuraf is the heavy odour of sweated garlic. From her seat in the back of the car, she can see part of the driver's face in the rear-vision mirror, his jaw grinding steadily each time he takes another clove from the small bowl on the dash, so when they finally arrive and she goes to get out she finds that her hair, her skin and her clothes have been steeped in it.

The first part of the trip is on a tarred road, a sort of highway with little traffic which is as well because all vehicles appear to travel at high speed in the centre of the road, moving across only reluctantly to allow oncoming traffic to pass. The sides of the road are littered with wrecks and with other vehicles that aren't wrecks at all, but which have rolled or skidded off the highway. Or merely run out of petrol and been abandoned – ironic, she thinks, given the number of oil flares that stretch to the horizon. There are no speed limits, no signs, and the road runs quite simply either due north or south. It is a case, she imagines, of there being few roads, so that as long as you are moving in the right geographical direction, you probably can't go far wrong.

Outside the towns, along the tracks and around the oases, colours blend one into another, muted pastels against a backdrop of ridged and tilting dunes and a soft Wedgewood sky. A mule moves stiffly, each leg in turn, under the slight weight of a white-bearded Arab who wears a patched robe of orange and turquoise stripes and whose sandaled feet almost touch the ground.

From time to time they pass a group of tents, a television aerial sprouting from each. A prideful mast of modernity, the very incongruity of which shouts the unease of this moment in time. She wonders if all the programs are broadcast in Arabic, wonders what you would watch if you were a nomad in a tent. What things become important or critical? What stories would you want to hear and watch? What stories would you be given the chance to hear and watch?

The driver turns sharply onto a road that is little more than an unmarked track clinging to the edge of a small oasis town. A suddenness of dark green made so by the abundance of vines and vegetables, of fruit trees and grains that mass and tangle in the shade under a grove of palms. *This* she must capture.

She fumbles for the Pentax, touches the driver lightly on the shoulder.

'Please stop.'

As she winds down the window, the hot air races in. She rolls out the zoom, adjusts the aperture and then, finger on the shutter, pauses to rest the camera on the ledge of the open window.

What is it that causes her to stop? She will wonder later whether it was Poppy's injunction, the slightly tart tone of her voice as she said, *The first thing to understand about this country is that it's a privilege for you to be here* that stops her. But now several thoughts collide, and uppermost among them is the realization that no camera can do justice to a scene like this.

Where is it safest, this image hovering in front of her? In a photograph album protected by a page of decorative tissue, fixed for all time, so her children can say: She was there once, my mother? Or in the album of her mind where some small trigger might bring back the context of this moment: the rush of dry heat, the bitter aroma of garlic, the struggling air conditioner? What is the best archive for the story behind the story: that of this city girl, this foreigner, sucked back to a time almost biblical?

How reliably will her mind hold the image at the centre of this scene, the sparks in the black eyes of the young girls at the oasis, their dark veils shadowing the prettily embroidered gowns of pale blue and green and pink, their movements both coy and shy as they fill goatskins with water from a well? Will she, at some distant time, still be able to hear their light, careless laughter? And see the mischief settle slowly over their faces as a sharp shout from above draws their gaze upwards to where a youth in his white robes is shaking fruit from the crown of a date palm. And behind all this, over to one side, in the lens of her mind will she be still able to recall this two-storey building of mud brick, the top floor on such a slope that surely the furniture will have to be anchored? And will she still be able to see the contrast between the dreaming on the face of the worker and the speed of his actions as he moves like a crab down the network of bamboo scaffolding to the ground. Will she remember the hammer he holds absently in one hand as he lingers on the last rung, his free hand rubbing at his chin, his gaze on the girls?

But a photograph? How much of this can a photograph capture?

She lowers the camera. An impossible task. The fixing solution would confine the scene and like all prisons suck it dry. A moving camera perhaps, but that would also have to zoom in and out, and it would have to tell this story of the boy and the group of girls and how they all looked and yet didn't look at each other. A painting might lend it more fluidity, but how much then of herself would become part of the scene? In the end is there any bank save the mind – precarious though it is – which can hold a picture like this with any degree of honesty? And even then?

'Take someone with you,' Dekker had suggested earlier. 'Make it a great deal easier to get around. Particularly the first time.'

Afterwards she sees that he was right in many respects. Negotiating the strange disordered city would have been easier had Poppy come too. And already each of her two trips out in this strange land have yielded more than she would ever have thought possible. But now her eyes are wet as she lowers the camera, rolls up the window and asks Mr. Kim to drive on.

It's dark by the time she gets back home and Dekker is waiting for her. He looks particularly smart, she thinks as she reaches up to kiss him.

'I've had some amazing experiences. There was this oasis…'

'Dana. The Bairds' tonight. Remember, hey?' He pulls at his cravat impatiently. It suits him, she realizes. He has the height to wear it.

'Yes, yes. I know. Trip longer than I thought. Won't take me two ticks.'

She races into the bathroom, washes her face and hands, steps out of her day clothes. There's a party this week every night but one and it's getting rarer to cook in the evenings, more a question of making a sandwich to soak up the punch or parry the effects of the wine. The beer is fine; I will stick to beer, she promises herself. She rips the label off one of the two floor-length caftans she had bought in the town, purchased for their modest neckline and long sleeves, but which she thought would also be easy to slip on and move around in. She shrugs into the paler one, runs the comb through her hair and flips it up into a French roll. A few Kirby grips later and she is back in the lounge where Dekker is pacing.

He gazes at her, a look in his eyes she hasn't seen there before. As they walk out of the house he runs his hands down her spine, over the curve of her bottom.

'You look good tonight,' he says. 'Nice frock. The yellow suits you, contrasts your dark hair.'

Blazing lamps and thumping music; the party announces itself from the end of the street and inside the gathering is swinging. Jim Baird scoops ice cubes into a glass with one hand, plunges a soup ladle into a bowl of pale yellow liquid swimming with slices of orange, lemon, lime. He presses the drink into her hand, shouts across the din.

'Matches your dress. New recipe Ali dug up. Made it myself so I can recommend this one. You know everyone, don't you? If you don't, just introduce yourself. And Ali's in the kitchen if you want to see what she's up to. I need your husband for a moment.' He turns to Dekker. 'Beer for you?'

Ali smiles up at her as she enters the kitchen. Dana has met her once before, a woman who has a bit of the schoolteacherly about her, someone who presides over her parties with a tight smile as if her guests are a class of rowdy school kids. She is expertly slicing a rectangle of cheddar into small squares. It's quieter in here, a little.

'Told Jim you'd come. D'you want to give me a hand? Bit behind the eight-ball here. These need stabbing, cocktail sticks in the drawer there, usual thing, mix of cheese with olives or pickled onions. Jar of gherkins if you need it. Then impale them on that melon there. Tried to get a pineapple, should have known better. Just need to get a bit more food into this mob. Though the way they're mopping up that punch, no amount of piccalilli is going to make tomorrow's dawn any kinder.'

She helps Ali with the snacks, fills the remaining platters with nuts, pretzels and salty crackers. She hears Dekker's laugh in the other room, knows he is enjoying himself. Leaves her drink behind as she rejoins the crowd, the plates held high in front of her.

Relieved that she no longer has that first-day-at-school feeling when she arrives at one of these camp parties, she stops here and there to chat and greet. Jim is right: she does know most people including – she spies at the back of the room leaning against a screen talking to one of the draftsmen – David Devenish. She has been relieved that she hasn't run into him since the incident on the hill; she had heard he was on leave. She slides her eyes away too late, flushes hot when she's not quick enough, when he looks up to meet her falling gaze.

Although she keeps her back to him as she makes her way through the crowd, she is aware first of his eyes on her and then increasingly conscious both of her will in this matter and her body's contrariness, its response to the silk slip under the filmy dress as it sucks and slips against her skin.

'Charming waitress tonight, I must say. May I?' In the end, he is in front of her. He fills his palm with nuts, raises his eyes to hers. His face is not quite tanned, but coloured by something other than the broken capillaries over the cheekbones and nose as if he's spent time in the sun, or another session on the *jebel* perhaps, and she is close enough to detect the sweet-sour smell of white spirit on his breath.

She lifts her chin, goes to turn away, but he nudges at her sleeve, his voice low.

'Hey. Wait a tick. About the other day. Sorry. Afraid I couldn't help myself. I deeply apologise.'

Pointedly she looks down at his hand still touching her arm. She lifts the plates higher.

'Please.' His voice drops even lower. 'We're going to run into each other constantly at these things, so how about we just decide to move on from the bad start? My house is at the end of the next row from here. Number 8. You can see it from your driveway. If you find you have a bit of spare time and want a chat, drop by anytime and I'll make amends for my bad behavior. Cross my heart. Want to be friends?'

He looks like a kid pleading for candy and for a moment she is distracted so the plate holding the melon tips and the spiked fruit starts to slide. His hand moves swiftly to steady it just as she steps back so firmly that her heel lodges in someone's shoe. By the time she has set down the platters, apologized and disentangled herself, he has moved away. When next she glimpses him he is deep in conversation with one of the engineers and she feels foolish and, for some reason, confused.

She looks for Dekker, but he is at the other side of the room with his arm draped loosely across the shoulders of a woman almost as tall and fair as he. Dana has started to weave her way towards them when Dekker laughs again, a full-throated laugh with his head thrown back. The blonde jabs him playfully in the side and whatever they are sharing makes of them an island in the wash of sight and sound so Dana turns away instead, gathers some empty glasses. A short while later he is behind her in the kitchen.

'Oh, so that's where you are,' he says, relief in his tone. 'For a moment I thought you'd gone home. Nice party, eh? Good crowd of people.'

'And the woman you were with? I didn't get a chance to meet her.'

'Anna? You haven't yet met Anna?'

'No.'

'Silly goose.' He pulls her towards him and she thinks for a moment he is about to kiss her, but instead he yawns and glances at his watch. 'Seven in the morning will come soon enough. Get some shut-eye.'

Dekker is snoring lightly almost immediately, but she finds it less easy to turn her back on the day and it replays itself backwards in a series of the snapshots she had been so reluctant to take. Dekker's head thrown back in laughter more spontaneous than she has heard for a long time. The tall blonde at his side. Devenish and his apology. The *sid* that had gone so quickly to her head. The shop where she'd tried on the dresses, bending almost double to hide herself behind a chest of drawers as she pulled the gowns over her head, the female shop assistant shielding her from the street, casting nervous glances at the open doorway. The acrid pungency of the garlic. The young Arab clambering deftly down the scaffolding, pretending an ignorance of the charms of the young girls in their jelly-bean-coloured gowns and to the covert glances they threw in his direction. And then Dekker again. His happy laugh. And that's because you haven't been here to hear it, she chides herself. From somewhere on camp comes a muffled tap-tapping.

She tries first to read and then to sleep. Finally gives up on both and lies with the sheet pulled up over her breasts, her book resting on her drawn-up knees. The hammering continues intermittently. It's work on the boat being built over on the other side of the camp, she guesses. A hell of a project that, building a boat in the middle of the desert. She wonders where he gets his material and his tools, whether they have all come from home, what he thinks about as he fixes each plank to the wooden skeleton. Where will they travel when it is complete, he, his gamin-faced wife and their two children? Where will all come home? She smiles as she remembers the pieces of bark with leaves attached as sails that she used to set into a muddy furrow to race against her father's. She never won, of course. But she tried.

Relieved that her mind is moving away from the incidents of the day, she reaches again for the light switch and as she does so the sheet falls to her waist and she sees herself in the mirror opposite, her long dark hair falling about her breasts. With one hand still raised to the light, she is still staring at her image when the rapping comes again, nearer this time, so she starts. A short series of knocks and it is then she senses the sound is closer than she'd thought at first and that there is, in fact, someone standing outside the window alongside her bed, someone looking at her reflection in the mirror across the room just as she is doing.

She starts to tremble even as she forces herself to keep her face neutral, her movements slow. She switches off the light, moves her hand under the bedclothes to gently shake Dekker's shoulder. Woken from his sleep, he is about to snap, but she holds her hand lightly against his mouth.

'Dekker. Dekker. Wake up. Quiet. There's someone. Looking in. Outside the window. Looking in...' She begins to shake, forces herself to sit back against the pillows, not sure whether she is overreacting, thinking in some muddled way that if this is true, if indeed there is a prowler, a peeping Tom, then there must still — despite the lack of light — be some reflection in the mirror. Dekker is awake as rapidly as he fell asleep. He, too, is naked and he slips out the other side, crawls around the foot of the bed to the bathroom window, stands to fling it wide.

His shout is more like a roar, something primal that rips into the night, makes her leap from the bed. She circles like a wounded animal on the answering scream that rattles the darkness. Another whoop, a sound of scrambling, Dekker's breath as heavy as her own.

'Gone. If only I'd had some clothes on. Could have caught the bugger…'

So there *was* someone, she wants to say, there really was someone looking in. The camp with its ten-foot wall feels so invulnerable she has difficulty believing it. Her fingers tug on a housecoat and she rushes through to the lounge in time to see a figure disappearing between the houses in front.

The next morning there are prints, sandshoe prints, just under the window. When she tracks them, they lead to the wall. But here, at the base of the soaring blocks of concrete, the tracks join the scuff marks of millions of identical prints that dent the damp morning sand.

TEN

'So what've you seen of the country so far?' He is already back in his car, door pulled shut, while she waits at the passenger door, so his words are lost. 'Ah, sorry, quite forgotten how to treat a lady. This do you?' He leans across, flings the door open.

'I was just asking,' he said as he reversed out. 'What you've seen of the place so far? Been any further than the *suq*?'

'Since last week? Yes. Yes, I have. I've been up to al-Dhuraf.'

He says nothing further until he turns through the gate posts of the Dutch camp and she likes that. Enjoys the thought that the chill in her tone matches his. Likes to think she is punishing him for something – for his boldness, his presumption – and that her small revenge is somehow made more solid in the silence. These bridge evenings are, after all, his idea. But she feels she coped quite well with the cards the previous week and it has been a good opportunity to get a glimpse of another compound – the houses here like real homes snuggled into their patches of garden, all of which are quite verdant, with some a mass of coloured blooms.

'I should have told you last time,' he says as he turns the key to silence the engine. 'My bridge system – the system I play – is Precision. I think it was Blackwood's you used last week. Something of that nature. But have a go at Precision. We might do better.'

'But I thought you said…'

He stops half-out of the car, one foot on the ground. 'At this stage, all you need to know are the openers. That'll give me a good idea of what you've got in your hand. One club'll tell me you've 16 or more points, one no trump that you hold 13-15 high card points. Right? The one club is forcing. Stick to that and don't be too clever and we'll do all right.'

'And I thought you said this was a social game.'

'It is,' he said, shutting his door with some force. 'But it's not tiddlywinks. It's still contract bridge. With the general idea being to win.'

She hates the lazy amusement with which he flips a card onto hers, she hates that she notices his hands at all. He plays bridge as he walks, talks and drives, as if it all, all of it, life included, is nothing but minor diversion.

As he drops her back, he says. 'Bit better than last week. You need to work at it, that's all. Keep your mind on what you're doin'. My regular partner's back next week anyway.

Katya.' The name rolls off his tongue. 'So you're off the hook.'

She is about to walk off when his short exclamation stops her. He reaches to the rear of the Ford, retrieves a book from the back seat.

'Nearly forgot.' He holds the book out the window. 'This. I thought you might like to read this. Seeing as how you don't seem to be gettin' around much. Richard Burton. And I don't mean the film star. Give you some idea of how this part of the world works. Difficult to get good reads here. Anythin' half-decent is passed around. Hand to hand.'

Taking her hesitation for politeness, he gives the book a shake.

'I've finished it. So there's no hurry to return it. Or bother to return it at all for that matter.'

She steps forward to take it. 'Doesn't anything mean anything to you?'

'Not much. Some things, yes. But not much.'

ELEVEN

Irritatingly, he's still in her thoughts the next day, the way he holds his cards low, close to his chest, so his eyes too are veiled and he looks half asleep. The lids blinking slowly like those of a sunstruck lizard when she makes the wrong move, the almost imperceptible tilt upwards of his chin when the cards fall as he wishes.

She shakes her head, sets her thoughts towards the day. It is eight o'clock on a Thursday morning and the men have been at work for over an hour. She has an uninterrupted four hours – three and a half before she has to get lunch – before Dekker comes home. Enough time to get started.

She has already pulled the canvas down from where she'd stashed it on top of the dining room dresser and it leans against one of the high-backed chairs in the dining room. She is back in the bedroom taking the oils from the bottom of the drawer, her small pots, tubes, brushes, when she thinks she hears a sound. She pauses half-crouched, lifts her head, catches the unmistakable click of the front door latch. Swiftly she moves out into the hall.

'What the…'

'Hello. The other night at the Bairds' place. I saw you but we didn't meet.' Already inside, the woman steps forward her hand outstretched. 'I'm Anna Modigliano and I'm lonelier than hell. Can I come in?'

Dana shakes her hand briefly, but the woman pushes on past. Slinging herself onto one of the dining room chairs, she glances back over her shoulder. 'Help. Help-help.' Her voice is surprisingly deep. She sounds as if she could be American. And yet not quite. Canadian perhaps. She starts to forage in the oversized handbag that hangs from a strap over her shoulder, gives up and drops her head.

For a moment Dana doesn't move. The woman talking so closely with Dekker. The Anna he didn't introduce. Footsteps on the road outside. Until she closes the door. She once saw a small bird perched in the fork of a tree, a leg on each branch, and it occurs to her that right now she feels like that bird. She resents the intrusion but she's not quite sure how to move forward. But it's not only this that stops her. It's the position of the woman who has come between her and the canvas. It is her lowered face, screened in part by the fall of her straight hair. The winter sun streams in low and full so it prints her picture on the canvas ready-made. A half-picture. Part-woman. The part-woman who was having such a comfortable chat with her husband two nights ago. As Dana continues to stand unmoving, Anna turns her head to one side, to face her, so her eyes shine green as the shallows of the Saudi sea against the different shades of sepia: her olive skin, the brown-gold length of hair, the sand behind her head. But then she looks away, sighs, and it doesn't look as though she intends to move.

Dana goes to put on the kettle; she wishes the woman had not come, but she has, and when she returns Anna is still sitting almost exactly as she left her with her elbows propped on her knees, her hands cupped under her chin, gazing out across the sand.

As Dana sets the tea in front of her, Anna turns to face the room. Her eyes flicker as if the sun has slipped behind her eyeballs, her fingers pick at invisible threads from the fabric of her long cotton skirt. She makes an effort to straighten her back, crosses one leg and then the other. She takes a deep breath, nods at the canvas.

'*Tabula rasa*. Blank-anything scares the holy shit out of me. Is that what you do with yourself? Paint?' Whatever spell she has been under breaks and she disentangles the straps of her bag from her hair, searches among the contents to pull out a pack of cigarettes. She screws up her face as she lights up, picks a strand of tobacco from the tip of her tongue. 'Still prefer them filtered, but this is all they had. I really don't know why I don't just cut out the smokes and chew baccy. Sorry. You?' She pushes the pack towards Dana who shakes her head.

The difficult timing of the intrusion. The difficulty of the intrusion altogether. She wonders whether Anna expects an answer. The canvas hangs over the room like the Wizard of Oz. She feels out of place, displaced in her own home. She should throw her out; she can't throw her out. No reason. She hears herself speaking.

'Well, no, not exactly. I don't paint. That is, not yet. That is, this is what I'm going to do to fill in time. While

I'm here.' It sounds so lame, lamer still in the face of the other woman's rejoinder.

'To fill in time? Fill in time.' Anna's nostrils flare. 'That's what everyone here is doing. Filling in time. Can't anyone think of something more original to do? How does one fill in time anyway? Will it stand still long enough for you to fill it with anything? Is it a bottle or a jar or a pot or a sack that it can be filled with something? Or does time only live outside space?' Her sentences come out thick and choppy, so for a brief moment Dana wonders whether she is smoking something stronger than tobacco. 'Why do people play so fast and loose with time? Something we only value when it's gone or when there's not enough of it. Or damn to hell when there's too much.' She draws deeply on the cigarette and then her head swings in search of an ashtray as she cups her hand under the curve of ash. 'Do you have something for this? And one day it will be gone. Time. What will you do then? Like Dorian Gray, will you wish it back again? Or is that why you plan to paint? In the stupid hope you can stop time right here?' Her gaze circles the room; with her free hand she fingers a necklace at her throat, a string of turquoise stones that looks wrong against her green eyes. She sees Dana's glance. 'South America,' she says.

Dana pulls an ashtray from the back of the sideboard cupboard, sets it in front of the woman.

'I'm confused,' she says. 'You bolted in here saying you needed help. And then?' She straightens her back, folds her arms, tries to hide the antagonism she feels by softening her tone. 'Exactly why are you here?'

'I'm sorry. So sorry. Shouldn't have gone off like that. Not your fault. But everyone here, simply everyone – all the wives that is — that's all they're doing. *Filling in time*. They talk about filling in time as if it's as infinite as the salt in the sea…' It's taken up to now for Dana to realize that her eyes are rimmed red. 'What a waste. What a waste for all of us. Me included. Don't you think?'

Break the flow, Dana thinks. 'Where do you come from and what did you do?' Realises only when the words are out of her mouth that now she, too, has absorbed expat-speak.

'Italian-American. But then I married a Brit. Hair threw you, didn't it?' Her face twists, not quite a grin. 'Part of the Nordic migration to the new land. As for what I used to do.' Her hand closes on the necklace as if she might rip it. Instead, she stabs out her cigarette, picks up the packet, taps out another. She draws deeply, blows out a cloud of smoke and when next she speaks, her voice is calmer. '*Did*. You know, it's almost impossible to reconcile its being in the past. Anyway, I was a television reporter in Hong Kong. On the face of it, it — that is, the crowd I worked for — operated as a normal commercial channel by subsisting on ad revenue, but strangely I always saw it as more of a welfare organization. Alongside all the news and normal sitcom shit, we'd slip in what we called exposé stories.' She shakes her hair off her face and leans forward. 'That was my area, you see.'

'Go on.'

'I can't really say what it meant to me. That job. There aren't words for it. All sorts of rackets we uncovered: dope rings, kid prostitutes eight-ten years-old, triad gangs, sleazy finance rackets. We worked in teams, research, interviews and so on. My role was to interview.

'It was dangerous sometimes, yes, but it was also power and you'd get the equivalent of a hard-on from that. All the stuff, you know. Fancy hotel rooms with big bowls of fruit, flowers, bubbly, boxes of matches with my name stamped in gold, complimentary massages. Wining, dining, dancing and falling into bed with the last waltz. Being met, farewelled. Lots of movement. The whole glorious deal. I was only a cog. I know that. An ordinary old cog, part of the whole. But we worked together well. We achieved heaps. And we did a lot of good.' She picks up her cup so suddenly that the liquid sloshes and with the cup still on an angle, she glares.

'I doubt you'd recognize the me of then in the woman I am now. I dressed differently. I had a different walk. I was decisive, good at what I did. And now?' Her laugh light as wind chimes unsettled by a gentle breeze. 'And now I'm Gerald's wife. That's why I'm here. I'm Italian aren't I? Family comes first. It's more than tradition; it runs in the blood. Double whammy.'

She spreads her hands, opens wide her eyes. Her voice drops to a whisper. 'And nobody, nobody...believe me, absolutely fucking nobody...understands.' She sets her untouched cup down on the saucer with a clatter, flings herself back at the chair, ash bending at the end of her smoke.

Dana searches for something to say. But what can you say to someone who, like herself, made a choice, but unlike herself, regrets it? She has the feeling that Anna will use a cleaver on anything platitudinous or soothing, and meanwhile she doesn't give any indication of noticing the passing of the present time. But then maybe she doesn't regard this as wasted? Maybe this is the help she needs? Maybe, just maybe, she doesn't consider Dana's mute company as feeble as she herself feels it to be? Some instinct has held her back from saying anything at all. Because she is scared for the statue that sits to one side of her profiled onto the canvas. The sun strikes at the glass door. She hasn't thought to switch on the air conditioning and a thin bead of sweat lines Anna's top lip.

'But why are you here?' Dana asks for the second time.

'Why am *I* here? In this goddamned dump of a place, you mean? Why are *you* here? For that matter.'

'No, that wasn't quite what I meant. I mean, why did you come *here*? To my house. My home. Today.'

The woman stubs out her cigarette. Jabs at the ash.

'I suppose I wanted to meet you.'

'And now you have.'

'Yes, and now I have.' Anna looks at her watch and rises in the same motion, then bends to gulp half the contents of the cup, sets it back in the saucer so the china sings. 'I have to run or I'll be late. Thanks for the drink.'

Once she is gone, it's as if she's sucked everything out of the space and that it will take time for everything to float back.

Patches of scum scale the insides of Anna's cup, her own drink not even sipped. She touches the side of her teacup. Still too hot. Smoke still rising from the ashtray, more ash, somehow, than the short visit warrants. She gets to her feet, screws up her nose as she picks up one of the stubs and presses it too hard into its own ashes, takes the tea things back to the kitchen. A moment later she is back, marching towards the canvas. She pushes her finger into the ash and starts to draw a face, a half-face that in the next moments becomes a trembling shadow on the piece of board. Here's one for you, Dad. She looks up at the ceiling. A real bitie.

When she runs out of ash, she sits looking out at the patch of sand and, just beyond that, the back wall of the house in front. No need for this to be bare sand. She will start to build a sanctuary just like the gardens on the Dutch camp.

'Good girl. I see you've finally started.' It's two hours later that Dekker returns for lunch, stops to stare at the canvas. And then his gaze swings sideways to the ashtray. He wipes his hand over the lower half of his face, rubs his hands together. 'Ah, and I see you've had a visitor?'

'Yes.' The word hangs.

'And she was? Or are you going to keep me guessing?' He smiles at her as if he is seeing her for the first time and it is only then she realizes that this is what has been missing between them. It is his attention that has been absent since the meeting at the airport.

'Anna.'

'Anna? What on earth was Anna doing here?' The disbelief in his voice and the look on his face is so comical she wants to burst out laughing. She is breaking up like badly-fired pottery. Is this hysteria? Is this the onset of a bout of hysterics when you feel two opposite emotions simultaneously? Her own laughter shrills in her ears. She wants answers to the questions she is unable to ask. But perhaps there are no answers. Or perhaps it is the questions themselves that have no validity. She is unable to meet his eyes for fear she will fall apart. For fear he will say it's true. Or that it's not true.

'There's lunch,' she says. Pointing.

'Dana?' he says.

'It's all right. On the table in the kitchen. I'm not hungry.'

His eyes follow her as she picks up the canvas, steps up onto a chair and tosses it back on top of the dresser. He comes up behind her as she walks into the bedroom.

'You think something's been going on. Isn't that it, eh?' His voice pitched a little higher than usual.

'Well.' She flings herself on the bed, folds her hands over her belly and stares at the ceiling. 'It's odd, that's all.'

'Odd?' He sounds as though he can't believe he's having this conversation. As if he's looking for the oddness in the word odd.

'Just the way she was suddenly here. She just – let herself in. Walked in. As if she owned the place.' Why does her voice sound like torn cardboard?

He sits on the edge of the bed. Pinches his eyes. 'She shouldn't do that. That's not right. She's got a lot of confidence, that's all.'

She rears up. He's sitting on part of her skirt and she wrenches it free. 'Confidence! So that's what you call marching into someone else's house without so much as a by-your-leave?'

He sighs and she doesn't know which is louder, his sigh or her breathing. They sit in this type of silence for a while. She hugs her knees. 'Confident. Yes. That's one way of putting it.'

'You could have asked her to leave.'

'I did. In the end, I more or less did. She just blew in and blew out. But I still – well, you know, it's still horrible. Having someone walk in on you like that.'

'I know. But try to forget it. She's just an unhappy woman. It happened. And now it's finished. We'll lock the door from now on, what do you think?' He puts his hand on her shoulder, gives it a gentle shake. 'Eh, Dana?'

'Let's get some plants.' She's not quite sure why she comes out with this a day or so later and the words surprise her as much as they do Dekker, but once they're out, she knows this is what she wants and why. It's not a garden she wants so much as a no-go zone between the house in front and their own. An empty space that will allow her to spill out of her box onto a segment of sand that may not be quite her own, but will not be anybody else's either. Less openness and more privacy, a filmy screen between herself and the rest of the camp that is not a separation as much as an amber light that flashes an if-you-please.

'Plants? What for?'

'A garden. I think I'd like to make a bit of a garden. Something green to look out onto, something lush. And to provide a bit of a screen between us and next door. More privacy. With a sort of patio area leading out from the house perhaps.' The garden grows as she talks. She stands very straight, her hands clasped in front of her.

'A garden? Lush? Here? Man, you must be joking. Lush and desert!' He shakes his head. 'Frankly not worth the trouble. Anything you plant in this sand and heat will die. Straight off. You don't know how hot it gets. This is the Arabian desert. Remember?'

'I know, I know. It sounds silly.' She stops. He's frowning when she would rather make him laugh – his full-bellied laugh. She shakes away the image, pushes on. 'And it's clear no one else on this camp has done it. But this compound is brand new and plants grow well on the Dutch camp where they've had a bit of time to get established. They have some really lovely garden spaces over there. So there's no reason why they shouldn't grow here, is there? Besides we don't know for sure it *won't* work. Couldn't we just try? Someone said something called the Green Garden has plants for sale...'

'You have to make work for yourself, don't you.' But his voice is less irritable. 'And I suppose we need to cart back all the manure and something resembling soil, too.'

'No. Apparently they don't need soil. Just straight into the sand.'

'Don't need water either, I suppose. Just exist on plain air? Right?'

'Need water. Some. It's not work. I'll do it. It's an ideal time. The weather is still cool. You're off tomorrow. Friday. Can we go then?'

'On a Muslim holy day? More sacred than Sunday so I doubt they'd be open. But the next day. I'll take leave and we can go.'

TWELVE

If, as the ancients believed, bad weather is a portent of impending disruption, the sudden sharp change in the atmosphere and the *shamal* that followed should have been warning enough.

The night after they visit the plant nursery, she tosses from side to side in the big bed, her feet seeking out cool spots in the sheets, her mind refusing to let go of the day that followed on from the three-hour drive to the small fenced-off oasis of cuttings and small plants.

'A choice of two – bougainvillea and oleander – and they certainly know how to charge. And without roots I'll bet,' Dekker had said as he'd stuck his finger into one of the small tubs of wet sand. Back home, he'd leaned against the door jamb as she scooped out a shallow trench around the area she had marked out as her no-man's-land, watched as she pushed the cuttings firmly into the loose sand, as she watered each from a glass jug. His annoyance burned into her back as she worked. It was muggier than it had been for weeks and the flies stuck to her as if she were paper maché still wet with glue.

The glasses of syrupy apple juice that passed for wine at dinner had been a bad idea. She lies awake, cannot rid her mind of the sight of the neat rectangle of grey sticks with the little plumes of green leaves at the top that resembles a rather ugly miniature stockade. Which she can't help thinking rather pleases Dekker.

When at last she falls asleep she dreams it's raining, a downpour pounding on the roof, rattling at the windows and then she wakes and the sounds fades, comes again. She lies rigid, holding her breath and listening for the tap-tapping of the prowler. Dekker is sleeping heavily and she raises her head to look at the clock his side of the bed, sees it is well after six-thirty in the morning. She must have slept for longer than she thinks, but it is unusually dark. The noise comes again, above her head this time, a distinct clattering now like a troupe of Irish dancers that wakes Dekker and they both jump out of bed at the same time. Outside, the other houses are blanked out as if by a heavy fog. It hasn't rained in al-Khasi for seven years she's been told. But now it's raining, raining hard. The rain tips out of the sky in globules, big and bold as camel tears. And then, as they watch, it dries up as suddenly as it arrived.

Two days later, when the sun has baked the sand back to its normal shifty crystals, the wind comes.

What strikes her first about this dust storm is its colour, a pale-grey cloud tinted sulphur-yellow. And then its fury: it is as if the world outside is possessed. The spaces between the houses form tunnels for the wind that roars and snorts – scooping, lifting, dropping, gusting, teasing the sand so it spins like a dervish. She closes her ears against the desperate haunting moan that rises and falls, so close to the keening of a household in grief that she shivers, hopes it is only the wind. The sand batters against the roof and the windows, whips the puny leaflets from the new plantings.

Progressively throughout the first morning of the storm the men filter back to camp from the work sites. Dekker prowls the house from end to end, a man pacing the parameters of a prison cell. It is, she guesses, a bit like being confined to barracks, at home with nothing planned, nothing to do. All you have to do is enjoy yourself. She wants to suggest this. Is surprised at herself and bites back the words.

It's early afternoon and they are in process of moving from lunch to siesta when over the racket she thinks she hears someone at the front door. She backtracks towards it, noticing without quite believing the sand that is sliding in under the bottom of the door, piling in little drifts in the hallway. She is about to reach for the doorknob when it's flung wide and she is slapped backwards against the wall.

'Steady, there. Steady on.' An arm shoots out to break her fall; Dekker is suddenly behind her and between the three of them they heave the door closed where it rattles as though it's holding back the Chinese army.

'Hope the lock holds. Sorry to do this to you.' A short round man with a shock of ginger hair who grimaces, takes from his pocket a large cotton handkerchief, wipes the sand from his eyes and dabs at the specks of blood appearing on his face. 'Ugh. Gotten sandblasted. Sharper than glass that stuff. Just as well this cloth is red. It means that spring is on the way, the *shamal*. Might even get more rain.' He holds out his hand. 'I'm Laurie, by the way, probably more widely and popularly known as Poppy's husband. Mind if I come in?'

You're in already, she thinks. But without waiting for an answer, he limps past her into the lounge. She wrinkles her nose at the sour smell he leaves in his path. 'Why are you here? Why are you out in this storm?' She wants to ask this, but the whistling scream that surrounds them makes conversation impossible.

Dekker has more luck when he mimes drinking, so she leaves them to their beers, heads for the bedroom. She clasps a pillow over her ears to block the rising pressure, to mask the incessant howling, swings her feet onto the bed and draws her knees up to her chest. But with all the clanging and whistling, it's like trying to sleep in an engine chamber. She reaches for the book Taylor lent her, opens it randomly to find Burton, too, at the centre of a desert storm. A *simoon*, he calls it '...the flaming breath of a lion...the upseething atmosphere, the heat-reek, the dancing of the air upon the baked surface of bright yellow soil...' So that's what it is, she thinks, that strange nicotine-yellow colour she had observed. The sand in the sky. She rolls onto her back, reads on. Burton is on camelback, travelling with a caravan of pilgrims, trekking across the Nejd desert towards Mecca. He dares not drink because *if you drink you cannot stop*; many of the pilgrims die from heatstroke or exhaustion, and attacks from bands of robbers are frequent and deadly. Richard Burton and Isabel, T. E. Lawrence, Jane Digby – they all experienced this.

Such courage, she thinks, or is it something more and something less – a mix of daring and nerve – a derring-do that's vanished with the times. And here I lie all disoriented when in reality I couldn't be more snug and safe. She stretches out her legs, rests the open book on her stomach. At this stage Burton would have been about thirty-two; he had met his Isabel, but had yet to commit to marriage. And yet, when he did, he could not have found a mate more suited to his own adventurous personality. She stares at the ceiling. All of life, everyone's lives, no more than a game of chance.

She wakes much later because she is cold, goes to pull up the covers and realizes from the half-light that it must be late afternoon. In the lounge she finds the two men as she left them. Or almost as she left them. Dekker is leaning back in his chair, eyelids drooping, his drink barely touched. Laurie talks and waves his glass. His beer slops. The storm wipes out his words, but perhaps it doesn't matter, because by now they form a meaningless monologue. In front of him on the coffee table are three large bottles, empty but for the lees.

Is it her entry or is it because the dusty veil over the sun is causing night to fall even more quickly than usual that causes Laurie to stumble to his feet? He nods at her, and she follows him as he zigzags towards the hallway. Outside the gale is unabated. His body doubles into the wind and the sand blasts in as she struggles again with the door. A metal bucket barrels across the sand towards him; he sees it coming, tries to sidestep, but hampered by the amount of alcohol he has consumed, he is no match for the wind which swings him back the way he has come. He struggles helplessly, floundering in figures-of-eight until abruptly he drops to his knees and starts to crawl. She looks back at Dekker, but he has closed his eyes and when she gazes out again, Laurie has disappeared between the houses.

Why did Laurie come today, through this gale, when he hasn't been here before? Is it for the companionship? Or for the drink? The wind howls and she can't help thinking of Poppy working away in a house just like hers. Doing what? Bathing her son? Reading? Writing up the minutes for one of her committees? Or just lying, listening to the storm, wondering how many storms lie ahead before she accompanies Rufus back to England and school? Or will she send her son to boarding school like many of the others? She suspects that Poppy, too, despite her efforts, will always be divided.

That night she thinks she hears the rain again. Fairly bucketing down, slamming onto the tin of the roof in the middle of the night. Sloshing about the floor of the dining room, rising from her ankles up her legs. She watches powerless as the chair first and then the table tilt and leave the floor to float in the swirling water, sway like ducks in a bathtub. From across the room, she sees her easel tip, on it a painting, any painting, it doesn't matter which. But then it does. Then suddenly it matters a great deal. As she heaves herself towards it, the water so high now it sucks her backwards, she sees her father reach for the board. He catches it deftly. Turns to smile at her before he looks back at the painting and as he gazes she sees his face change first to one of astonishment and then of dismay. He looks across at her. You don't try hard enough, he says, holding the corner of the canvas between thumb and forefinger. Battling towards him, half-wading, half-swimming she holds out her arms for the painting, but just as she reaches him he drops it and by the time she scoops it up, the canvas has sagged like a dishcloth. The water that swirls around her is dark, dense. It must be from the ink, she thinks; the bities are bleeding. Or the floors. It must be that the floors are dirty.

She struggles upwards, steps out of the dream. Her nightdress is sodden with sweat and the pounding on the roof is real; the rain has indeed started again. She rubs the sand from the corners of her eyes, turns on her side. She doesn't remember going to sleep but she must have been reading because when she finally wakes the book lies open on the floor.

The men are back at work and the winds have eased enough for her to walk across the camp, book in her hand, to where the single men are quartered in rows of transportables the other side of the compound. She knocks, a hollow echo that bounces back at her from the metal door of the cabin.

'Uh. So you decided to come did you.' He steps back, swinging the door wide, but she is unable to tell from his face whether he is pleased or annoyed.

'I didn't think you would be here. I thought you would be working? I was only going to leave this. Return this. It was handy having something to read through the *shamal.* Thank you.' She holds out the book to him.

'Shift work. I don't work the same hours as most. What can I offer you? Coffee? Tea? Scotch?'

'Scotch? How on earth did you get hold of that?'

'Dutch camp. Stuff's trucked in. Massive containers. Bacon, ham. Straight-up pork, too. It might surprise you to know. Meant to be under-cover. But of course everyone knows.' He shrugs, moves back another step, opens the door wider still. A small ceremony. 'Welcome to my house.'

He doesn't quite bow, but there is something grand in his gesture, something between humility and pride or perhaps a mix of both. An animal, all senses engaged, challenging her to enter his lair.

She stands uncertainly. There is a point always, a moment in time when you stand balanced between two choices when it's as easy to move forward as it is to back out, always that moment which in retrospect becomes *the* moment, a fulcrum on which you stand on tiptoe knowing things are about to change, but not how or what or why. Besides, she is not quite sure why she is here. To return the book, yes. Put the book down on the step and leave. Why then did she bother to knock? Why not just leave the book? Is that what he is thinking? He jerks his head, pulls back just slightly, as one might test for life at the end of a fishing line. There is always the moment you can step back, she tells herself again. And then there is that moment when it is too late.

'I'm not sure I should,' she says, finds herself moving forward, stepping up into the metal cabin to stand in the small space. Again, she holds out the book. Awkward now. When he makes no attempt to take it from her, she places it on a chair. He closes the door behind her and she is surprised to find the cabin quieter than the house. Dimmer too. Quiet and dim like a cave.

'Well. What'll it be?'

She looks at him out of a tumbling confusion, wanting to stay, wanting to leave.

'Look, why don't you just relax, lady? I'm not going to jump you. Sit down and have something to drink and make an old man's Saturd'y afternoon.'

She shrugs, decides. 'Scotch and soda, then. Drown the Scotch please. I like a long drink.'

'This is not one of your city bars, love. It's a camp in the middle of the desert. I've a bottle of the former, but no soda. Sorry. Soda on top of good Scotch is sacrilege, anyway. No one ever tell you that?' He breaks the seal on the bottle, splashes it into a small tumbler which he fills halfway with water.

'Sacrilege or not, that's how I like it. Drowned, I'm afraid. With lots of soda. It's just the taste I like.' Copying him, she bites into the words and sits to balance on the wooden arm of the chair, wondering as she does so what exactly it is about this man that put her so quickly and fiercely on the defensive. And what it is that causes her to be here anyway? Returning the book? Every nerve in her body presses her to gather in her self-respect before it is too late, to make some excuse – she'd only come to return the book after all – and to back off down the steps. But he comes out from behind the kitchen counter, steps towards her, the drink in his hand.

'Well, I'll make a point of gettin' in some soda then. Meanwhile.' He presses the tumbler into her hand. 'Water do you?'

'That's rather presumptuous,' she protests. 'That presupposes I'll come again.'

'Well. I hope you do. What've you seen since we last spoke? Got out and about yet?'

'Yes. No. Not really. We went to some place called the Green Garden to get some plants.'

'What sort of plants?'

He is bored, she thinks. 'Oh, just oleanders. White. White was all they had. And no roots, just sticks really because the storm took care of the few leaves. But they say they'll take.'

'They will. Give them water. That's all.'

'But in this sand? How?'

'The salts in the sand. Makes them grow quite well. Surprisingly. And with spring coming on they'll sense something in the air too. Won't be long before they're reasonable size bushes.'

'So you don't think they'll die then?'

'No reason to. Only if they don't get water. Give them three months. Three months and a bit of tlc. Everything responds to that. People too.' Into the silence. 'What else you b'n up to?'

She sips the drink, glances across at the book. 'Well, reading of course...'

'As I said. Not many good books to be had in these parts.' Although he is stretched out in the other armchair, his eyes half-closed, she senses the opposite. The push and pull in him. That he's strung tighter than she, taut as a piano wire.

Opposite her is the print of a painting, a nude woman astride a silver horse. She looks away quickly. Takes another gulp of the drink. His mouth twists a little.

'You don't come across as the shy type. But. Bachelor's privilege. That's a Salvador Dali there. His Lady Godiva. Should swap it for the Lautrec in my bedroom. Been thinkin' I might play around with some paints myself one day.'

'Me too.' She closes her mouth on the words, but they are out before she can stop them. She looks quickly down, not ready yet to discuss the work that is not yet a work.

But instead he says, 'I'm going to Hofuf on We'nsd'y. You might like the ride. It's a quaint old town…' He pauses because she is laughing so much that she slides herself from the arm of the chair onto the seat. 'Gone and said something funny have I?'

'No. Not funny. More unfunny. It's just that I wonder whether every man here is going to offer to show me the sights.'

'Uh. Bad experience?'

'Yes, well, um…it could have been bad. It was certainly unexpected.' She pauses and then when he says nothing, adds. 'And unpleasant.'

'It's a question of having your wits about you. Same here as anywhere in the world. You want to think about Hofuf anyway. Get that husband of yours to take you. Like I was about to say it's a lovely old place. Easy enough to get to from here. And there's a bit of a legend about it, quite apart from the old buildings. Some say it's the burial place of Layla and Majnun – certainly their tomb is there.'

'Layla and Majnun?'

'Majnun. The mad one. There I was forgetting you've only been here a couple of months. So you won't know the story of the lovers. There's a good book about them you might come across. Star-crossed love, and ain't it always like that?' He sticks his tongue in his cheek and for the first time she imagines she sees a flash of humour in his narrowed eyes. 'Anyway Majnun – or Qays as he was then – wanted to marry Layla and her old man wouldn't allow it.

Or so legend has it. So he went mad with wanting her, wandered around in the desert for the rest of his life.'

'That's the problem with love. Once requited, it ceases to exist. It's like thirst. Or hunger. Once satisfied, it's no longer there. It swallows itself.' But even as she speaks, she wonders whether she believes this. It could just as easily be the opposite – you could drown in it – like the line she had read again from Burton's book. Something about being so thirsty that once you started drinking, you would never stop. Perhaps that amounted to the same thing. But he is nodding.

'Sometimes,' he agrees. 'It can certainly be like that. Romantic love anyway. Plenty of warnings in the ancient tales. Tristan and Iseult. Romeo and Juliet. Or, like I said just now, Layla and Majnun. Thought it would appeal to your romantic side. I'll see if I can track down the book for you.'

She shifts uncomfortably before the immobility of his body, the stillness of his eyes that haven't shifted from her since she stepped into the room. She imagines herself trapped on the surfaces of his irises and the image repels her so she drains the glass too quickly.

'I have to go. I just wanted to return the book.' She walks across to the kitchen counter, sets down the empty glass. 'Thank you. Thank you for the drink.'

'Thank *you*. For livenin' up the afternoon a tad.'

Afterwards she finds it hard to remember what his room was like except it was fairly bare. Everything quite clean and washed up as if he were expecting visitors. There was a fringed rug, a couple of armchairs, cushions, the print on the wall. With him sitting opposite and asking questions, telling stories. But in all, in some strange way, it was rather splendid.

THIRTEEN

It is a full day later that the winds drop away completely, that the sand stops falling out of the sky and the clean-up starts. It isn't just the grit in the house with the ceilings bulging from the weight of it blown in under the eaves, the small ridged dunes in the hallway, the sand piling in the corners of the windows, it's the sand you can't see that's worse, she says out loud. The day before she had stripped the bed, swept the bedroom twice, but throughout the restless night the sheets had still felt like sandpaper and the grit still clings to her feet and fingers, invades her mouth, her eyes, her ears. Outside, the sand has settled thickly on the floors of the small porches, crept up the sides of the houses. The maintenance guys are busy crisscrossing the spaces between the houses with shovels, rakes, blowers, giant vacuum cleaners.

The desert reclaims its space and quietens down quicker than I do, she thinks, still unable to dislodge the ghoulish wailing from inside her head mixed somehow with the rising water in her dream. And my poor plants, headless and buried to their waists. Should have listened to Dekker. Can't get rid of the whine of the wind. Every time I see Taylor he asks whether I've got out or where I've gone. Sounds like I'm in jail. Perhaps I am. Perhaps I should *get out* more. There's the car. And the driver. Before I know it, I'll be back home and say I went to Arabia. Everyone will look at me: Arabia! What did you see? What was it like? What did you do there? And what will I tell them? The *suq*, yes, I saw the *suq* – and I can pronounce it too. And the oasis, the pretty girls in their bright gowns. The plant nursery that sells sticks with heads of leaves. The *shamal*. But mainly this camp. So neat. An ordered collection of prefab houses built on their squares of sand, and around it all there was this massive wall of concrete blocks. All duns and browns. Or grey. Not gold. Where's the gold. Strange him saying he wanted to paint. I could have asked him more about it. I sat there in his room locked up like a schoolmarm. Can't get rid of this dust. Fast as I wipe it, it settles back. Must still be in the air. Probably dump for days. Wonder why Laurie came the other day. And how Poppy has fared cooped up with the kid for three days.

She wanders back and forth with broom and duster, wonders about getting out her painting before she decides there is not enough time before lunch. In the end she throws herself on the couch, her eyes hot and full.

She decides to visit Poppy. Make lunch and then go. Quickly she butters bread, can find nothing in the fridge but tomato and a heel of cheese, so she slices this up with a little pepper and salt, sandwiches the slices together, cuts them neatly in half and covers them with a damp tea cloth. Pretend it's ham and tomato with loads of hot mustard, toasted and buttery. Pretend I'm in my lunch break at the canteen. Pretend I'm meeting a friend at a ritzy café. Or dispense with all that and pretend I'm a vegan. But then there's the cheese.

Someone has made half an effort with the sand on Poppy's porch, scraping it roughly to one side so at least the door opens. Evidently the maintenance crew hasn't made it across to this part of the camp yet. She stands waiting for a minute, knocks again.

'Hello… Poppy, are you there?' Her voice echoes back. Must be collecting the child from playschool. She is halfway back to her house when she remembers there is still no playschool on the camp. But still, a hundred other reasons as to why she might be out. Nevertheless she swings back and, placing her feet carefully in her original tracks, returns to the sandy porch.

When again there's no answer, she tries the handle, and is surprised when the knob turns easily in her hand. She opens the door a fraction, calls out and stands for a moment to listen, lifting, tilting her head. She is about to pull it to when she hears a child's voice; a door at the end of the passage opens and Rufus comes running out. She bends down, her head level with the little boy's face.

'Where's your mother? Where's Mummy, Rufus?' She raises her voice. 'Poppy?' But he's tugging at her skirt so she follows him into the gloom of the passage, down its length, longer than hers, to where Poppy is propped against the pillows in her bedroom.

'Aren't you well?' She pauses in the doorway as if there is a boundary there, as if stepping over the line is something that has to be sanctioned.

But Poppy waves her in and Rufus climbs onto the bed.

'Come closer. I heard you earlier – at the door – but can't shout, talk much. No energy.'

'What's wrong?' Dana frowns. This isn't the woman of just a few days ago who circled the camp for signatures and then went to the Resident Engineer to campaign on behalf of them all for more facilities, for a schoolroom for the children complete with someone qualified to teach, for a library, and for a hall where they might watch movies or play billiards or table tennis. 'What's happened?' she asks again. 'Is something up?'

Poppy shakes her head. But then why does it look as though she has been crying? Why is her face so sharp, her jawbone a harsh triangle, the area under her eyes a transparent blue?

'Oh Christ,' she says, pulling a damp handkerchief from under her pillow. She presses it hard into her eyeballs, blows her nose. 'Promised me I wouldn't do that. But it's...Rachel, you see. I think I'm going to lose her.' She presses her lips together and then crams the cloth into her mouth which fails to smother the high keening wail. It is as if the storm of the past days is being reborn through her.

'Lose her? Rachel? You mean, the baby?' Dana steadies herself against the door jamb. She feels dull, as if she isn't here at all, as if this is no more real than the rising waters of her dream. She should be doing more than stand about asking stupid questions as if her mind has been stolen by the *shamal*. Poppy is whispering. Dana crosses the room quickly, leans over the bed.

'Could you…would you…do me huge favour? Could you get me a towel, two towels, from the linen cupboard and then take Ruf to play in his nursery for a few minutes. I'm bleeding, you see. Quite badly. Don't want to get out of bed. Don't want Rufus to see.'

'But you should be in hospital. You shouldn't be here on your own like this. With a small child. Where's Laurie? Why isn't he with you? When did it start? Does he know?'

'Knows. Please.' She shakes her head. No more.

Dana brings the towels, takes the child to his room and it's as if she is seeing him for the first time: a small boy with uncertain eyes who, apart from his red hair, doesn't look like either of his parents. She pictures him an early reader, a boy who will wear black-rimmed thick-lensed glasses very young. Sitting in a chair too big for him as he hides behind the covers of a book that he is really too young to understand. A boy who will fulfill his own predictability by moving from boy to man quite smoothly and without surprises. As she riffles through a raffia basket full of toys, she wonders why she sees him this way. Why not as boisterous as Laurie, as persuasive and strong as Poppy? Is Poppy strong? She hopes she is.

She sits cross-legged on the carpet, pulls out a box of Lego blocks. He stands in front of her watching the movement of her fingers as she starts to build the foundations of a home that will be square and true and quite different from the neighbouring houses – and built on something other than uncertain sand. Then he wants to have a go.

'Okay. You do it then. Build a house for me. Build the walls and we'll finish it together. I'm just going to check on your Mummy. You stay here and work on it for me.'

'What colour?' he wants to know.

'Blue,' she says. 'Or yellow. Or how about both, a mix of blue and yellow. Then we can use red for the roof.'

Back in the end bedroom, Poppy hands her a bath towel. She takes it, willing herself not to look at it, not to think, not to… Poppy's hand nudges her.

'Please. Put it in the bathroom. Bath. Laurie'll wash. Close door 'cause of Ruf.' Poppy's hand pushes at her again and still she stands there, not believing this, not believing the transparency of Poppy's wrist, the weight of the sodden towel.

But the bath is full of such towels. She drops it in the bright thin carmine of the bathwater with the others, pushes it in deep, tries not to see the clots swim free. How much blood is there in a human body? Eight pints she thinks she remembers from somewhere, from school biology. A goodly proportion of that must be in this one towel. How much can a person lose before it becomes dangerous? Less than this, she guesses. A lot lot less.

She checks on the child who is still absorbed in the building, fills and brings a glass of water to the bedroom.

'What about something to eat? I can make something. Or bring it over. Or fruit? Anything? And Rufus? Should I make him some lunch? Do you…want to go to the toilet?'

Poppy shakes her head, gives up an attempt to lift her arm to look at her watch, tries to smile, gives up on that, too.

'Laurie home soon. Thank.' She closes her eyes.

Dana returns to the boy's bedroom. The least she can do is to keep the child occupied. While she waits for Laurie. He should be home for lunch. She can't imagine what's in his mind, in his head, leaving his wife, leaving *anyone*, let alone his wife and child, alone in these circumstances.

The house has progressed to ceiling height. She proposes a second floor and when this is in place finds two larger sheets of Lego that clip together to form a roof that overhangs the walls rather too much, touching the carpet on either side so it looks like something the seven dwarfs might inhabit. A bitie house, her father would call it.

'Never mind,' she says. 'I think what we need now is a chimney, don't you?'

'But this house doesn't have a chimmy.' He looks around the room, up at the ceiling.

'No, not this one. But in England they do. And you come from England, don't you. Don't you remember your house there having one?' He shakes his head slowly and she remembers he must have lived here, in this house in its sand patch, almost all his life. Perhaps he was born here. She explains about fireplaces and chimneys and although she senses his lack of understanding, they build three.

'It's a house with lots of places to keep warm.' She smiles at him. Or lots of fire. Lots of excess.

There is no question in her mind but that Poppy should be in hospital.

FOURTEEN

'You speak to him then! It's not right, Dekker. It's absolutely not right.' She stares hard out the window at the car reversing out of the driveway opposite.

'Keep your hair on. It's not up to us. It's a private thing. Between the two of them. Don't get involved. You have no right to interfere and you'll regret it. Besides, perhaps it's for religious reasons.'

'Religious reasons! Someone like Poppy! But she's dying. Can't you see, I'm trying to tell you she's dying. She's lost a ton of blood and she's weak and hardly able to speak. She's about to miscarry. If she hasn't already done so. And he's not there. For Christ's sake, Dekker. *Laurie's not there.* He's out working. Or drinking.' She rounds on him. 'Like he was the other day. I can't believe he left her like that in the middle of that ghastly storm. Came over here and just drank and drank. Oh, and he was already drunk before he got here. I can't believe you won't talk to him. I can't believe lots of things including the fact that I've given up my life to be here in this godforsaken place to be with you and all you do is immerse yourself in your bloody magazines or attend darts' parties.' She takes a deep breath. 'Religion. Pah. What do you think they are? Jehovah's Witness?'

'Or Catholic. Look, I've had just about enough.' His eyes narrow, slivers of cut glass. 'You can't blame him for wanting a bit of company. Cooped up with a sick wife and young kid for two days… And what is this about giving up your life? You had the choice of coming here or not coming. The decision was yours, Dana.'

'Is that what he told you: that she was *sick*?' For a moment she is unable to speak. They glare at each other.

'There was nothing he could have done for her even if he had been there,' he continues evenly. 'And he was only a couple of houses away. In her condition, rest is the best thing. As usual, you've blown everything out of proportion…'

'That's what you'd do, is it? Let's leave out for the moment the fact that he's played at least some part in all this…in her *condition*. If I was miscarrying is that what you'd do? Leave me with the kid, go off for the afternoon to visit your friends? Or, as in this case, people you hardly know? And, yes, I came here because this is where you want to be and I wanted to be with you. But that doesn't mean…' She forces a breath, grips her hands hard together. 'Please Dekker. I beg you. We have to do something. We can't *not* do something. It's not as though there's a hospital on site. He'd have to take her to Dammam or al-Dhuraf or wherever it is they have a hospital. An hour, two hours' drive. Or maybe there's not one there either? And she can't even sit upright. She's fucked, Dekker.'

For answer, he picks up the bottle opener from the coffee table – an ugly implement fashioned from the cloven hoof of some dead animal that they'd been given as a wedding present and which she had never liked – and she hears clinking as he forages around in the store cupboard for one of the large green bottles. When he returns she is sitting with her chin in her hands. She watches as he drips the ale carefully onto the inside of the tilted glass. The colour of mahogany, she thinks. Dark brown tinged red with just the faintest of fairy froth that looks like scum sitting on the top.

He is about to take a sip when he brings the glass away from his lips. 'You know what the problem is with you?'

'No?'

'You're nuts. In this case. You're crazy if you get involved in something like this. If you think you're doing anyone a favour by coming between a man and his wife, you're nuts. What is it, Dana? You have everything here – all mod cons – to make things easy. People ready to be friends. What is it about you that you can't just get on with it?'

The house too small for her body and her skull too tight for the hurricane that roils inside. Quite suddenly she finds herself outside in the uncertain light of late afternoon, striding cleanly between the prefab houses where the children are building sandcastles, carefree as only children can be.

The straight line she takes leads her to the high wall around the compound and she doesn't stop even then until she feels it hard and sharp on her hands, her eyes a nose-length away from the roughcast concrete, too close to see anything but fuzzy grey.

But you, Wall, are only a wall, she whispers. And the fact you are a wall does not make this camp a prison. How can it be a prison when I came here of my own free will and when I can leave at any time? And how can I be so ungrateful to want to be free of it all when all I have to do is enjoy myself? Why is that so difficult? So hard to do?

The wall sags away from her so she holds her clenched hands up to it, takes pleasure in the pain of her skinned knuckles.

All these things you have, replies the Wall, *like the washing machine with the spin inbuilt, the super-size freezer that snaps and crackles when you lift the lid, all manner of crockery and glassware including glasses for champagne, sherry, wine, port and liqueur in a country where the consumption of alcohol is illegal. And remember how you always wanted real leather furniture? Well, now you've got it, although you never thought about how it sweats on the days the cool air fails. And marble floors that grow streaks that won't come off no matter how hard you scrub and scrub so you cheat with the precious drinking water because the saline leaves smears…why are you crying…when this is your proper job now to keep the house clean and your husband happy and you are doing an appalling job of both. When you could be building a nest, working on your painting technique…And friends – the friend you've made – how well are you doing there anyway? For goodness' sake! Any other woman!*

Away from the even hum of the air conditioner, it's cold with a whippy breeze that carries the chill of winter not quite spring. She feels it first on her neck and cheeks and then too suddenly on her bare arms, through her body. Taking her hands from the wall, she folds her arms hard against her breasts.

Her brain clears so she eventually sees herself standing brittle as a vase fashioned in the era of Ming, a bit crazed and shivery, with arms crossed and eyes still angry, but sad too. Why can she not be satisfied? Maybe she *is* going mad. Mad as Qays.

The last of the day is snatched by the sinking sun. Outside the wall, it would be shapeless, an ugly red balloon sucked into the sand. The sun, always the sun. Somewhere, somewhere in all this, a moon is rising. It is just that the wall is so high she cannot see it from here. Her nails bite into her palms as she turns to face back the way she came.

The following day she crosses the camp in a different direction.

'I was hopin' you'd come again.'

Partly to conceal the unexpected warmth his words invoke in her, she turns away to close the door. He limps back to his chair.

'What's wrong with your leg?'

'Ran into something the wrong way in the aftermath of the storm. Gashed it a bit, that's all. I was the moving object. My fault. I've had worse.'

'Can I see?'

'Keen to make a fuss over me, are you? I won't stop you. It's b'n a long couple of days.' He stretches out his leg. 'What brings you anyway? After another Scotch? Bottle's in the cupboard under the sink.'

'No, not Scotch. But I'd love a cup of tea. I could make one for us both.' Gently she kneels to peel away the bandage to see a wound long and deep enough to gape a little. She draws back, looks up at him. 'It really needs stitches, wouldn't you say?'

He shrugs. 'Too late for that. Rest it, that's all.'

She looks at it critically. 'It looks quite clean, but it could probably do with a new bandage?'

'You might find something in the bathroom. Yes to the tea. Help yourself.'

It wasn't so much that the rest of his house was as neat as the front room. It could hardly be otherwise being practically empty. Only a partition to separate the bedroom from the living area and around this, the narrow bed with its army-issue blanket stretched tight and a single pillow. Nothing, not even a book, on the bedside table. Just another print of what looks like a cabaret dancer on the wall at the end of the bed. In the bathroom, a razor and a bar of soap, a towel on the rack. In the cabinet, a half-used packet of Aspirin. It's as though Nobody himself lives here.

'There's nothing there,' she says coming back into the room. 'You knew that, didn't you? Why didn't you save me the trouble?'

'I'm beginning to cotton on to the fact that you don't believe anything you can't see for yourself.' He shrugs again, rubs his hand across the stubble on his chin. 'Besides I rather like having a woman stompin' round the place.'

'You know nothing about me,' she says as she rewinds the bandage over the wound. 'And anything you'd guess would be wrong.' She stands. 'There. Given the fact you don't even have a basic medical kit, that will have to do for the moment. Where's the kettle?'

'There's a saucepan I use, the small one. Left of the bottom cupboard.'

She fills the pan, sets it on the stove. 'And the tea?'

'There'll be tea bags somewhere. Or if you're after the loose stuff it's over your head and there's a teapot same place as the pan.'

She can feel him watching her from the chair in the dim corner, his gaze following as she moves about the small space. Like Rufus, she thinks. But unlike Rufus, she senses he is watching more than the movement of her hands. She wonders at his opening comment. Had it sprung from politeness? Or at the prospect of relief from boredom? And why should it matter to her one way or the other?

The boiling water fizzes and spits up the sides of the pan as she tilts it to splash into the teapot.

'Some bitchy saucepan you've got here. What's with it?' She takes him his mug. Leans against the counter to take up her own.

'Cheap tin. Aren't you going to sit down?'

'Wouldn't you prefer me to stand? Isn't that what the men on this camp expect? Or would you like me at your feet. On the floor, like this?' She flings herself on the carpet, her back against the other chair, glares at the steaming liquid in her mug.

'On the floor is fine. You were happy enough to kneel at my feet earlier. Though a bit closer would be nice. What's upset you so much?'

You, she wants to say. But this isn't the place to lie. So she says nothing, concentrates on the coloured spots on the outside of the mug, wonders whether they're printed on the mug itself or on her eyeballs.

'Had a fight with that husband of yours I suspect. It was coming up.'

She wants to set down the mug, pictures herself setting it down so sharply on her way out through the cabin door that the liquid spills, the mug might even break, the pieces fall apart and the tea collapse into an ugly puddle on the white counter-top. It might even drip over the edge onto the carpet and he would continue to sit there gazing at her with his lips compressed and the faintest suggestion of astonishment in the crease between his eyebrows. She wills him to say one more thing, to make one further comment about her life or her character or anything at all that will give her adequate reason to loosen the remaining band she has on her control and allow her to snap in two, quite crisply, like a dry stick. Tries to imagine what it might be like after that. Whether there would be a caramel-like peace oozing from the centre of her, whether all this wanting and passion and the difficulty of wanting things to go back to the way they were and stay that way for all time would just leach away to where it could do no harm. She forces herself away from the silence in the van to the happenings outside – a faraway place punctuated by the sharp screams of children at play, the engine of a car switching to silence, one of the metal doors down the row opening and clanging shut, a mother calling. The camp has grown silent by the time she takes a sip from the mug in her hand; she imagines the children inside now, reluctant to leave off their games, sulky at first, warming as they relate the day's play to their fathers, as platters of hot muffins, butter and jam are set in front of them. The light outside fades and the cabin settles into dark, both the drinks long gone. She senses he hasn't taken his eyes off her the entire time.

'It's Poppy,' she says finally, knowing this is the truth, but aware that some part of her is still lying and that this is not the full truth and to tell only part of the truth is still to lie.

'And what's up with Poppy now?'

'Why do you say it like that?'

He shakes his head, moves his shoulders loosely.

'I went over to their place just now,' she continues. 'Earlier today. And she's in bed losing pints of blood. Literally. She has either lost or is in process of losing her baby. She's so weak she can't speak, yet she doesn't seem to want to go to hospital. Sort of gritting her teeth and sticking it out. I waited for Laurie. Tried to persuade him to take her anyway. I mean, they must have something resembling an ambulance here? But he's so weak that man, weak as in weak character…and he won't do anything either. She's going to die, Tay. She'll die if no one does anything. And Dekker…' she swallows. 'All Dekker can say is "don't get involved". *Don't get involved?* When someone's in danger of dying. I find it difficult to believe. I *can't* believe it…'

'Dekker's right. Like I said earlier, you don't believe anything you can't see. So I'm not sure you'll be satisfied to hear any reasoning from me either.'

She is aware of her hand closing hard on her empty cup.

'But,' he says, the word tipping crisply off the end of his tongue. 'But. In the event you're receptive to listening to a reason for something you don't understand, my guess is that she doesn't want to go to hospital for two reasons. Firstly, they'd abort the child to save the mother…'

'Here?' It is her turn to spit the word. 'Huh. Oh, really. I hardly think so.'

'Yes, here,' he insists. 'Even here. *Particularly* here. In Islamic law, abortion is an evil, that's so, but the mother's death is the greater evil. And – as you discovered yourself – she wants this baby. Very much. Secondly, there's a strong possibility that she's scared...'

'Poppy scared? I don't think so!'

His gaze doesn't flicker. 'You're not listening – a strong *possibility*, I said, that she's scared. You see, the baby is not Laurie's. Don't know how much they can figure from a foetus that age, but if it came out brown, for example, when its Mum and Dad are fair and ginger respectively, there could be a problem. If you get my drift.'

'What exactly are you saying?'

'I'm trying to get through to you that things aren't always what they seem on top. And that sometimes, in trying to do the right thing, you can end up making a right old mess of things.'

'Brown? You don't mean?'

'Brown in a manner of speaking. I think you're bright enough to figure it out for yourself. And let me just add that the penalties under Islamic law for adultery don't exactly favour the woman...'

'And Laurie? Why doesn't he do something? Do you think... You don't think he knows, do you?'

'I would guess he knows all right. Poor bugger. What can he do? And who can make a woman do something she doesn't want to do anyway.' He nods at the window, pushes himself up from the chair. 'It's been dark for some time. Don't you have dinner to cook. Back home?'

She scrambles to her feet as he swings open the door.

'I thought she loved Laurie.'

'This has nothing to do with love.'

'What's it to do with then?'

'It comes from having too much time to fill.'

'Just one thing before I go. How come you know all this?

'A camp like this is a big fat pot of soup sitting on a mess of burning sticks. And, remember, these are just *strong possibilities*. But. And here's something else you might think on. How would you like it if you were forced to go to hospital if you didn't want to? If you were forced to go anywhere you didn't want to?'

'If it were for my own good…'

'*Even if* it was for your own good. *Especially if* it was for your own good. If someone else made the decision on your behalf. Think it through.' He closes the metal door sharply behind her.

Dana waits a week before she calls on Poppy again. Their disagreement blown over, each day Dekker reports that Laurie is on site and she can't think even Laurie would go to work if something had gone seriously wrong. Besides, if the camp is the village Tay describes, she will hear any bad news soon enough anyway.

When Poppy opens the door, she looks recovered. Almost. No, not almost. Completely. But different. Instead of the usual caftan or flowing skirt, she is dressed in a pale cream trouser suit with a froth of lemon chiffon around her neck, an outfit Dana hasn't seen before. Poppy in trousers is a different person from Poppy in a long skirt though why this should be so Dana is unable to work out. Her thoughts run into each other. Poppy knows exactly how to team her clothes. She's lost the baby. She's thinner. But while the thinness becomes her in one way, it adds a frighteningly skeletal expression to her face.

She doesn't know how to look into what she knows will be the direct gaze of Poppy's grey eyes, so she notes other things. That it is getting hot. That the weather has been calmer in the days since the storm than in the period leading up to it. That the sand has gone from the single step. The path has been swept. The front porch looks normal. Spotless. Poppy spotless. She doesn't know what to do with her eyes.

Poppy takes her hand and sits, lowering herself with care onto the edge of the concrete floor of the porch. Holds onto Dana until she's forced to crouch beside her.

'You don't know, can't know, what it meant to me.' Words, whispers. 'Your coming the other day. To say thank you is not enough. And you know, Dana? Don't you? About the baby?'

'I'm so sorry.'

'Although in some ways.' Poppy kicks at the sand. 'Maybe it has to be like this.'

Dana holds her hand. Returns the pressure, measure for measure. There is no answer that comes to her.

FIFTEEN

Starting with the canvas had been a bad idea. Like trialling for the Olympics without the basic strokes. Too clean and cream and empty. Too publicly stark. Too public altogether as it had turned out. Over the last two days she has been working with pad and pencil, reaching sometimes for coloured crayons. Her jeans discarded in favour of light blue shorts and a white halter top, she lies on a towel within her rectangle of sand and allows random images to float across her mind. Those that linger she transfers to paper, stopping when the image passes, so for the first few pages she has a series of unfinished fragments, hieroglyphics almost, that hint only vaguely at what the images might be. Interspersed here are pictures more recognizable like the few leaves of a grapevine draped over a pillar or what might be a grassy plain with the wind stirring through it or a series of vibrantly coloured hoops of beads. Or a bus crammed with forty black figures and one white. A dog waiting at a window. And as she continues she realizes she is not sketching at all but writing in pictures. And that, she says to her father, is why the bities worked for me first off. Because they represented the impossible happiness of that day: me and my friends dancing in the sun. Having fun.

Could that be why her struggles to paint have failed? Is it the simple and yet impossibly complex fact that technique, persistence and determination can undoubtedly take you far and that talent can possibly be dispensed with, but one essential ingredient is the almost unconscious need to set it down. Not just to tell it or describe it because then it would linger on in the mind, but transfer the thought to something physical. A tablet, papyrus, journal, typewriter, canvas or sketch pad. Paint or draw or write the story out of the subconscious until the birthing is complete. And maybe, too, to do that successfully one has to reach for something deeper than desire – to where desire becomes *need*, to where there is a story inside that *needs* to be told badly enough to find its own energy. Some things, Dad, can't be forced. Not everything can be ordered. Or orderly. A story can't be a story without first seeing the pictures in your head any more than a painting can be a painting without an underpinning story. She knows now why in the life drawing class her nudes looked mummified, why her *plein air* attempts at trees and mountains and fields of flowers failed. She was *too* determined. Or she used that determination in such a way it became a negative. Sees clearly for the first time why she had been so successful at the museum. The answer when it comes is so simple: draw or paint, study or work from the inside to the outside instead of the other way round. What isn't clear to her is why she has taken so long to see it.

She lies on her stomach, chin resting on one fist. The sun is warm on her back, the flies not so bad today. Over the past couple of pages she has progressed from sketching the past to more detailed drawings of the present. Three Arab men huddled over their pipes, a small child looking on. The oleanders around her — new leaves sprouting fresh from the stems as well as the heads. A statue of a nude with her head buried in a block of marble whiter and brighter than a cloud wrapped around the sun. No heavy blue outline around the white-on-white, just a lightly pencilled body with part of the head buried in whiteness that stretches to the edge of the page. She asks herself the story of this drawing. Has the figure buried her head in the marble voluntarily or in distress or is the statue still a work in progress? Is she trapped or will her head eventually be cut out of the stone?

Her period had come that morning. Warm, redder than life, heavier than usual. When she told Dekker, they stood looking at each other and she was left feeling as if she'd taken a burning dish out of the oven in her bare hands with nowhere to put it down. Perhaps he was right and she was too tense. You should relax more, he keeps telling her. Lie in the sun, go gossip with the other women, why don't you, eh?

Under her hand now the profile of a face, the chin resting heavily on a bent wrist. The story behind this face tells itself in the narrow eyes open wide with horror. A private suppressed horror, a horror hidden until this moment of its awakening, concealed even from the person in whom it lives. Like Conrad's Kurtz. She tells the story behind the face in the puffiness around the eyes, the mobile mouth drawn thin and tight, in the wrinkles that await their stage call just under the surface of the skin, those lines that in the end are going to make the face less of a blank page, make it more interesting – tell the story of a life lived...

'I say. Talented!'

Dana starts, shades her eyes to look upwards into the sun.

'Anna!' She flips the pad closed. Her heart thumps as she scrambles to her feet.

'Sorry, didn't mean to startle you; you looked altogether too peaceful. But I hear you have a driver? Any chance of cadging a lift to al-Dhuraf?'

Dana looks at her curiously.

'When?'

Anna shakes out her hair, lifts her shoulders. 'Anytime. Whenever you're going.' She hitches her large brown shoulder bag higher. Her mouth twitches. Dana wonders how much of the drawing she's seen. Or if she'd even recognize the other Anna if she did see it.

'The day after tomorrow?' she says quickly. 'What's today? Tuesday? We could go Thursday. I'll ask tonight. But I'm sure it'll be fine. Leaving here around nine in the morning. Does that suit? If it can't happen, I'll let you know.' Or I'm sure Dekker'll let you know, she adds silently. And hates herself for her unfounded suspicions.

The tall woman gives a half-smile and a wave and is swallowed up by the rows of houses as quickly as she arrived.

Dana grimaces at the saplings. Grow hedge, damned you. As tall and thick and quick as you can. Or I swear I'll sing to you.

She settles back down on the sand but she feels ruffled as if the wind has started up again in some invisible place and then when she checks her watch she's amazed to find it's nearly the men's home time anyway.

'Can we talk,' she says to Dekker when they're settled in the lounge after dinner that evening sitting at right angles, one on each of the two sofas.

'Talk?' He's poised over his stamp collection, a portion of which is laid out on the large coffee table, his tongue resting lightly in the corner of his mouth. With as much care as he would take if it were a butterfly's wing, he lifts a stamp with a pair of tweezers. 'Yes, of course, shoot.'

'No, I mean really talk.'

He looks up at her and then back down at the stamp, moves restlessly. 'I said yes. What do you want to talk about?'

'Just, you know, talk.' She sees the beginning of a frown as he stares at the square of paper hovering in the air as if something about the stamp doesn't please him. 'You know, like we used to. Back home.'

'You're not going to start that again are you, Dana. For now, this is home.'

'It is. In one way it is. But also it's not. And things have changed. Between us.'

He stretches his back, shuts his eyes for a moment as if to clear his mind and then turns to her. He is still gripping the stamp in the small pincers. She wonders whether it will tear. Or if the pincers will break. Even pincers have their breaking point.

'Everything changes.'

'But us. We've changed.'

'It's what happens in marriage.'

'I don't want it to happen. I want things back like they were.' It's her turn to wriggle. 'This doesn't feel like marriage. It's lonely. I thought the idea of me coming here was so we could be together.'

'We are together. We are sitting together in this room.'

'I want us to be in love again. I don't believe that has to change. Dekker. Please. Talk to me.'

He sighs, gazes longingly at the stamp, puts it down.

'Your friend Poppy. Have you been to see her?'

'Yes, I have as a matter of fact.' With a little start she realizes that already another two days have passed since she called on her.

'And how is she?'

'She's actually quite well, to my surprise. Amazingly well. Considering. On the outside anyway.'

'Ah, you see. I told you! Leave these things along and they work themselves out.' He picks up his glass of ale and sips it. Toasts her silently.

'I don't feel I was a very good friend to her,' she mutters.

'So what did you do today?'

'Nothing.'

His frown is back.

'It evidently doesn't suit you to do nothing.'

'No, I totally agree. It doesn't. That's been my point all along, don't you see? I don't do stamps or seashells and there's only so many coffee mornings I can stomach, books I can order and wait weeks to receive, and then reading I can do… I'm bored Dekker. Bored out of my tree. Can we go somewhere. Taylor mentioned Hofuf was interesting, some ancient buildings. An old lovers' tomb. Perhaps we could go Friday?'

'Yes, you could certainly go to Hofuf. But why not go with one of your friends? Fill up the days you say are hanging so heavily. You always want to go rushing off somewhere and Friday is really the only day I have to relax.'

'But, together Dekker. I want to go with you. Do something together.' They both stare at the stamps. This is his prized East African collection, the animal series of the lion, giraffe, zebra and elephant each on a separate coloured background. Of them all it is the lion that that most appeals to her, a tawny-grey beast standing on a savannah plain in an orange dawn. Dekker looks across at her.

'Jesus, Dana. I don't think this is going anywhere, do you?'

'No.' She gets up. 'You're right. It's not. I'm going to bed. To read.' She's almost out of the room when she remembers. 'Oh, and I almost forgot. Can I have the car the day after tomorrow? I'm going to al-Duraf. With Anna. I said I thought it would be okay.'

'Anna? Why Anna?' She can sense a difference in his tone. A deliberate attempt at lightness. That fails.

'Because she asked me.'

'Anna asked you?'

'Yes. Goodnight.'

But he doesn't answer and when she looks back he is sitting slumped in front of his stamps and she wants to rush back in and put her arms round him. But something stops her. Something too filmy and intangible to know whether what she feels has any basis of reality.

Maybe I am going crazy, she says aloud. And then smiles at her mother's voice: The first sign of madness is talking to yourself.

When she gets into bed, she puts out her hand for her book, remembers that Tay had promised to search out Qays' story for her, turns off the light instead. Next time she sees him she will ask him to tell her the tale. Perhaps Poppy will accompany her to Hofuf.

SIXTEEN

How silences vary, and how inadequate the word is to cover all the different silences: when silence is stillness, when silence is resentment or bewilderment or companionable, when silence becomes white noise. Or when it's so quiet that noise becomes something you imagine rather than hear, like a baby crying when there is no baby.

But the silence that accompanies this trip to al-Dhuraf – this harshly framed hush with the sound of the engine and the drone of the air conditioner threading through its unbending awkwardness – is none of the above.

Just what had possessed her to agree to Anna's company? Although company is hardly the right word to describe the presence of this person who sits curled into a corner of the back seat, her face turned stiffly towards the window, so rigidly contained, perhaps, because for once she doesn't have a cigarette in her hand. For them both, why this drive? For Anna, is it time-out from her loneliness? For herself, is it just another excuse not to sit in front of her drawing pad hoping creativity will pop out of the sand like a genie? Or did her quick decision arise from some dark place in her mind? Was there a perverse desire on her part to see Dekker's reaction when she asked for the car? If Anna means nothing to him, she knows he will give no further thought to the day they spend together. But if the opposite is true...

But what of Anna's husband? How does he figure in all this? She has only met him once. A lightly built, rather indeterminate man whose only distinction was that he walked on the balls of his feet like a Siberian tiger. Not that she has ever seen a Siberian tiger – or any real tiger for that matter – but she is convinced that is how it would move, a little differently from a lion, more sinuously than the other big cats, sure and light on its feet. Apart from this way he had of moving, she remembers very little else about him. Not even his name. But perhaps in the case of someone like Anna it's appropriate that he be called Anna's husband instead of the other way round. Like Dekker's wife.

Her hands are damp despite the chill in the car. Clenched and damp. She glances at her watch. Not even halfway there. She wonders how often Anna has been up to al-Dhuraf. From the small rapid movements of the back of her head, it is not difficult to imagine her eyes moving back and forth, taking in the gas flares that flame on the horizon, the chimney stacks of the aluminium smelters, the wrecks to the sides of the road. But does the desertscape affect her? Does she too feel the soundless echo of the sand waves? Or are her thoughts less abstract, more reasoned, connecting more with small rushes of adrenalin – or prayers – that she will survive the current journey as Mr. Kim guns the Volvo down the centre-line of the narrow road? It is both possible and impossible to ask Anna these questions. That's right, Dana. You can't work out your own life, so why not take on someone else's?

They take a different route this time, so instead of the oasis they pass through two small towns, past the rather grand and sonorous injunctions of the hidden *muezzin* calling the midday prayers, the men flicking out their prayer mats and folding themselves into the shape of a zed with the lazy grace of camels. She is glad, suddenly, of the changed course. The sanctuary under the date palms had been so unexpectedly special, it would not have been right to layer it with the splintered ice of today. What will shopping together be like?

Again, the crassness of the town after the sleepy rhythm of the drive is sudden and brutal. Biblical blue and gold gives way to the harsher primary colours, to the red-and-white head-dresses of the men, the slate-black cloaks of the women. Where there was the *muezzin*'s call echoing across drifts of saffron sand, there's a metropolis with no right or wrong side of the main street. No right or wrong to any of it. Cars and trucks nudge each other with drivers powerless to do anything except hit horns, pump klaxons. Bicycles wobble through the web. A man holding a struggling goat in his arms leaps out of the way as patience snaps and one of the cars mounts the kerb. The other drivers come alive, keep their thumbs on their horns, stick their heads out of the windows, their yells suffocated by the noise. Alongside the muddy ditch that runs through the centre, a mule pulls an overladen cart, another reminder that just a short while ago this town was a village.

But for all this, there's something thick and releasing about the air as they step out of the refrigerated car into the sun. Anna smiles, a real smile that plays around her lips before it moves to her eyes. The fingers of one hand dive to retrieve her cigarettes; her straight hair glints gold as she shakes it out. Relieved this time at the sudden change, Dana finds herself smiling back.

'I need the bank,' Anna says. 'And you?'

'I'll come too. Any bank?'

Anna shrugs. 'Whatever. I need to exchange pounds for riyals.'

They find the bank quite easily, step through a brass-handled revolving door. Anna turns to look over her shoulder, raises her eyebrows at the unexpected majesty of it, at the way it occupies a space of seriousness in one of the few two-storey buildings in the town. An enormous painting of King Faisal of the House of Saud hangs opposite the entrance, dominates the room. What had she heard said about him? Good with finances, perhaps that was all. A double reason, she thinks, for hanging his image in a bank. Even if there is something off-putting about the angle of his beard. And the way his lips jut out reminds her quite suddenly of the immigration official. Not quite cruel, not quite kind. Four months since then, incredible that four months have passed already. Dekker at the airport. His warm *Don't stay away so long ever again.* And after that? Since then? She can't help feeling a little cheated. Sad, too. Expectations again. She shakes her head to clear it of the thoughts that had kept her awake most of the night. Perhaps Dekker is right and the onset of tedium and irritability is the normal pattern of people who live together for more than a few years.

She stares at the red carpet which covers part of the roughly cast concrete and then up at the long curving counter with its row of teller windows, a face in each, looking outwards into the huge hall, all of them quite still like paper cut-outs designed to resemble tellers. How unlike home it is, no queues of bored or impatient people waiting in line. And then Anna is back, well not back exactly, but walking straight past, not stopping, but pushing through the door. She yells over her shoulder as she disappears into the brightness. 'Go to the moneychanger, he says. He can't – read *won't* – do it. Over the road.'

In contrast, the squat ugly building across the busy street is more crowded than the trading floor of a stock exchange in boom time. No queue. Just a milling mass that reminds her of the airport.

At first they are just part of the throng, bumped and pushed so they are pressed up against each other. Anna swings her huge shoulder bag between her breasts and hugs it to her. Then someone spits, the shuffling silence becomes a murmur and they find themselves quite suddenly in the middle of a mass of angry men. A shout from somewhere and the crowd splits apart to leave them standing at the top of a long and empty aisle that leads to two men sitting behind a small table at the far end of the room.

It's only later that the details of those minutes come to her, that she feels the heat in her face as they are chivvied down the aisle with angry growls and short snapping gestures, her gaze fixed straight ahead on the money-men at their crudely carved tables with the brass scales to one side and the little drawers of money on their laps. It's only later she recollects the eyes, the rows of eyes on either side that sweep up and down and through her body. It's only later she remembers the riyals thrust into her fist and the panicky haste with which she and Anna stuff the notes into their bags, hasty as criminals with the alarm in their ears.

Back on the pavement, Dana takes a deep breath. She would like to do nothing more than sit somewhere quiet and dark, but the incident has the opposite effect on Anna who, with money in her bag, is set to spend. From shop to open-fronted shop she races. In a dark corner of one store, she pulls on caftan after caftan and, since they all suit her willowy blondness, buys the lot. About halfway down the street they stop to gulp lime juice from cracked glasses before heading off again to look for gold. In a backroom of one of the many jewellery stores, Anna selects half a dozen bangles, weighs them in her hand, slips them over her wrist. Inflexible circles of soft Italian gold that mirror her impatience, that jangle as she walks and shoot fiercely up and down her arm each time she gesticulates, each time she lifts her fingers to her cigarette, each time she tugs at her hair.

When Dana gets tired of following her around, she tells her she will wait. I'll be over there, she says, by the stream. Take your time. And feels her shoulders start to relax as she stands in the muggy midday sun. The gutter is running strongly and she wonders again where the water comes from. Pale brown, fast running and surprisingly full of fish. Masses of fingerlings, bright silver fish out-swimming the moving water. All around her is the Arabia she has come to see. And yet she stands in the middle of it absorbed by darting fish. Thought-free they are, she tells herself, emotion-free. Except. She looks more closely. Except that here and there, there is a fish that dares to swim against the current, battling upstream against the flow, deftly dodging the others. Why swim upstream against all reason? Stubborn? Addled? Lost? Or just the way it is?

She had decided that morning to leave the camera behind, to take her sketch pad instead, and she is searching for this now when Mr. Kim appears in front of her. He smiles his apology and points to the car parked a little way up the street.

'The madam is ready? The other madam…she all finish now.' She follows him to the car where Anna is snuggled up against the other door, her head against the window. She looks as though she is asleep and she doesn't move for the next two hours, doesn't wake until they drive through the gates of the compound. There's a moment during the drive when her head is the same angle as the half-finished sketch, starkly profiled against the background blur of sand. But her mouth is softer, oddly vulnerable. On the horizon, a gas flare.

SEVENTEEN

She is walking home from a game of tennis when the big green and cream car pulls up alongside. Tay leans his arm on the open window, sticks out his head.

'Hopin' I'd see you. Something that might interest you. The Dutch camp is quittin' its stock of English-language books. Was wondering whether you might think of doing something with them?'

'Doing something with them? In what way?' It's hot; her head is crowded with heat. It is too hot for tennis; they should start earlier in the day. She shades her eyes. 'Like? For example?'

'Well, like settin' up some sort of a library. P'raps.' He shrugs. 'You'd need to work on it quickly. I suspect. They need the space and the books are just in the way. I can get them delivered, but you'll need to get hold of a room somewhere to set them up. I was thinking Laurie's wife might like to give you a hand, at least in finding a useful space. She's got some influence with God?'

She raises her eyebrows. 'God?'

'The chief engineer.'

She glances quickly over her shoulder. And then wonders why she does so.

'Do I have time to think about this?'

'What's to think? You either can. Or you can't. I was under the impression you were after somethin' useful to do.' He gives a small cluck of irritation.

'I've got my painting. Remember?' She snaps.

'Ah yes. And there I was forgettin'. Well, so long.' He draws in his head, engages the clutch.

'Well, in that case. If it's that urgent, then, yes,' she says quickly. 'Too good an opportunity – I would rather ask Poppy first, but if they won't wait – then go ahead. Please. And thanks,' she calls out after him. But he has already driven off.

Poppy finds a space to set out the fifteen hundred books.

'It fits beautifully with my grand plan to actually get a schoolteacher on this camp. They've given us a house that we can use as part-schoolroom, part-library. How good is that!' She clasps her hands under her chin and then she crosses her arms and hugs herself, the sparkle back in her eyes.

'We can do this together. What do you think? Open regularly? For an hour on alternate days? Or twice a week? Every night? And we can catalogue them properly – you'd know all about that, wouldn't you? Hurrah!' She gives a little skip. 'And you know something else? We don't have a newsletter in this place. If we had some sort of a newssheet we could request that people leaving al-Khasi donate their books. Or, for that matter, donate them when they're finished with them. How about that!'

'How long should we let them borrow?'

'Three weeks? That's heaps.'

They do it together, a team of two, where just the kindergarten act of cutting up sheets of ruled paper and pasting them lightly into the front of the books to serve as a date page makes her feel strangely teary. For an instant she wonders at the emotion, wonders whether it's possible she is pregnant. A moment later she is absorbed into the routine. Most of the books are fiction and they debate whether to categorise them by genre or by author or by both. Poppy is convinced borrowers will go straight to their favourite author.

'But what then? We don't have so many books that it'll take them long to wade through their favourite names!' So they do both, writing out the first three initials of the authors' surname on appropriately coloured paper: pink for romance, red for adventure, orange for crime and yellow for the sprinkling of classical texts.

After the first morning, they stand back to look at the pile of processed books. Dana puts her hands on her hips.

'It's going to take a while. But I think that looks…well, quite professional don't you? And time, after all, is what we have.' She gives a wry smile. 'In drifts of Arabian sand. And in a way, this is as much for ourselves as anyone else, isn't it? So we want the whole operation to work as smoothly as possible once it's up and running.' She picks up a slim orange-and-white volume on top of the stack. 'A Scott

Fitzgerald and one I haven't read.' She runs her hand softly across the cover, continues more slowly. 'Poppy, I wonder whether the library will continue on after we've left the camp? Whether it will exist for as long as al-Khasi?'

'Yes, I wonder,' says Poppy slowly. 'I wonder a lot of things, but you can only live for the day, can't you? Otherwise.' She shakes her head. 'The trouble with this place is that people come for six months, a year, two years at most.

'Sometimes the men stay on, but look at those leaving in the next month or two.' She counts off on her fingers. 'The Bells, Pamela Innes, Jan Hunt and her husband, the Simpsons, Tiny is taking her son back to boarding school and it's my bet she won't come back, and the Korean lassie, forgotten her name, has already returned…'

'Cho-hee? I wondered why I hadn't seen her around…' She stops at the memory of her first night on camp, the pretty girl's hesitation – *Also not sure. My husband. He like very much here.*

'Yes, I didn't hear much about her going either. One moment she was here and then I called on her one day and her home had been allocated to someone else.' She stops. 'And those are only the ones I know about. There are lots of others suddenly no longer around.

'If they stay any longer than the norm, then they just stay on. Bit like us, Laurie and me. I can't work out whether they, we, are trapped or seduced – and in a way that can amount to the same thing. You know, you can rant against the loathsome restriction of prison, but if you're in for any length of time, you've got one hell of an adjustment ahead of you once you're set free. When I was with the legal firm, we came across some interesting – and frightening – stuff about prisoners who had served out their sentences only to find they could no longer cope on the outside.' She grimaces. 'Here, I don't know. I only know that some of us come and don't go. And that it's more than the money that keeps us here. But in my three years, I've seen a few get quite depressed or go a bit nutty in the process. Helps, I think, if you have kids.' And then she's quiet.

For the rest of the week, apart from random thoughts and occasional questions there's a rhythm to their silence which follows the pattern of their work. Poppy prints the letters in a clear, clean hand that reminds Dana of painstakingly chalked block capitals on a blackboard. She cuts out little squares of paper and tapes them to the spines of the books. Sometimes Rufus accompanies them, sits on a rug playing quietly with his toys and muttering to himself in between his half-hourly biscuits.

When they open up on the fourth morning, they find two tall sets of shelving, a small table and two chairs standing in the centre of the room amid the cartons and piles of books and once they heave the shelves against the longer wall, the room already has the makings of a library.

'Nearly done,' Poppy says. She gazes at the wall of empty shelves, the piles of books with their coloured tags. 'We've done pretty well I reckon, don't you?' She grins. 'They – the books – look somehow cheerful. Expectant.' They stand back to stare, clasp mugs of tea. 'I have to say that I didn't come across much in the non-fiction line. A few biographies, travel and that's all. It's strange there's not more on places to visit in Saudi itself. Look at this – Spain,

Portugal, Egypt, Turkey, Greece. Two on Greece in fact. Nothing on this place, not even the Emirates.'

'Well, tourist-wise, it's not happening here, is it? It's becoming increasingly obvious to me that we have our hands tied rather literally in terms of travelling about this place unaccompanied by a male. Six days a week, the men are working. On the seventh, they do what Dekker does, very little. Understandable, but...' She bites her lip. 'I guess, when you come to think about it, since it's the women who are going to use this library more than the men, simply because they have more time to read, perhaps it doesn't matter. Perhaps there's no real reason to have books on travelling around this country unless it's to point out to us wives what we're missing.'

'I hadn't thought of it like that. Reminds me, I feel bad. I said I'd go to Hofuf with you, didn't I? Totally forgot. Broken promise. Don't usually do things like that.'

Dana smiles and shrugs. She is about to speak when Poppy drops onto the seat behind the little table. She looks up, her eyes large and dark in a face still too thin.

'Promise,' she says. 'Solemn promise you won't share with anyone what I'm about to tell you?'

'Don't be silly, of course I wouldn't share anything private...' But then she stops, her mouth opening and closing on nothing like the big koi in her father's pond. Because as she stares into Poppy's eyes, she has a horrible feeling that there's nothing in them to indicate that Poppy's actually present. For all her methodical work, she looks suddenly and frighteningly absent. For an instant, Dana wonders whether she's on drugs, but surely she would have noticed? Wouldn't she?

But suddenly Rufus is at Poppy's elbow with his big clock and she starts. 'Good chap. Reminded me. Time for lunch. True confession has to wait. Next time,' she says to Dana. 'Tell you tomorrow.'

Later that afternoon she calls on Taylor.

'I need to thank you. *We* need to thank you. The library is real. It's going to make a huge difference. It's made a difference already.'

'Glad to hear it. Coming in for a cuppa? Water's just boiled. As it happens.'

'Poppy's managed to get hold of shelving and table and so forth, everything's categorized and labelled. Just got to actually shelve the books and we're ready to go.'

'Suits your methodical way of goin' about things. I can see that.'

'I wish you wouldn't presume...' She bites back her words, takes her mug from him. 'Actually very few non-fiction titles. Nothing on Saudi itself which surprised us. Which reminds me. It doesn't look as if I'm going to get to Hofuf in the short term and the book you mentioned hasn't yet turned up in our stock. So why don't you tell me the story?'

He sits to stretch out his leg, takes a sip from his steaming cup, eyes steady as she settles herself in the other chair.

'Thought I already given you the gist? Well, like many of the best legends, there are dozens of different versions of this, of course. But most of them amount to the same thing.

'Way back, you see, in the time of Muhammad, there was a young Arab lad, Qays they called him, who belonged to one of the Bedouin tribes in the far north. No one knows exactly where. And who knows what that part of the country might have been called before the mapmakers made merry with their quills. But it's a fair bet that if he's buried around these parts he didn't live too far away. As you probably know, up till quite recently the Bedouins were herders – goats, sheep mainly – true nomads travelling from place to place as the food sources ran out. But, progress was bound to find them wasn't it? And so now they're likely to lead lives as couch potatoes in front of their television sets…'

'I saw just that,' she exclaimed. 'Right next to the highway, a line of tents with television aerials! What would they watch? The news? Propaganda? Plays? I wondered.'

'Don't rightly know. That's something for you to find out. I suppose they have their Joneses in the desert too. If you get my drift.

'Anyway. If Qays had stuck with his old man's sheep, he would probably have been set. But his father had a few sheckles and the reputation to match and so he made the mistake of sending his son to school where he met and – or so the story goes – fell in love with the fair Layla. For reasons that've never been clear to me – because evidently the lovers were of the same tribe – when he did the right thing by the girl's father and asked for his daughter's hand in marriage, he was refused. Maybe there was a feud between the two families. Or maybe they had a wealthier match in mind, because she was married off soon afterwards. Unhappily. Of course.

'Don't know who came off worse. Qays left his tribe and wandered about on his own. From time to time he was spied writing in the sand with a stick or talking to himself. And by and by the writing became a collection of love verses. So. In time, along with building quite a reputation for himself as a poet, he went crazy for his lost love. Became known as Majnun, the mad one. But his poetry has stood the test of time. Along with their story. And – as I said earlier – the tomb.

'That's creativity for you. Nothin' like a bit of pain to seed it. How's the painting comin' along? By the by.'

'Why are you so bloody cynical?'

'I don't believe I'm cynical. More sardonic. Yes, sardonic describes me better.'

EIGHTEEN

She *should* stop her somehow, but how? This is Dana's dilemma when she hears Poppy's admission. But *could* she have stopped her? This is what she will ask herself afterwards. Later, too, it is Poppy's fingers flicking back and forth through the catalogue cards that she will remember, fingers oddly short for her long lean body, the neatly clipped fingernails polished with a clear varnish that might just as well have been red so vividly did they remain in her mind.

'What's up?' she asks finally later that morning. Moves across a shaft of sunlight to pick up another string of books, lays them out in alphabetical sequence along her arm.

'I've got a job,' Poppy says lightly, too lightly.

'You've got a job? What do you mean you've got a job? What sort of job?' Dana nudges her chin towards the half-filled shelving. 'More than this, you mean? A real, paid job?'

That was the moment the sun stepped outside the room, that the prideful books taking up their allocated places on the metal shelves looked exactly what they were: books people couldn't be bothered taking with them when they left for home. Dana feels slightly giddy. As if she's being asked to grow up too suddenly when she's in the middle of playing house. Being Mummy and Daddy to all these books, their precious children.

Poppy looks past her to the far wall. 'Mmm. Exactly that, in fact. A proper job.' When she turns her head, her face is so solemn, her eyes with such a strange unfocused cast that it is this, too, that Dana will remember later. But then the light changes again, some trick of the heavens; it shafts back through the window to catch at the reds and yellows in Poppy's hair, flickers in the nylon threads of her scarf, tied this morning too tightly so the knot pinches a fold of too-thin skin at her neck. Dana sucks in her breath.

'But we're not...allowed. You told me so yourself. Remember? *There's a ban on wives working. Working outside the home, anywhere beyond the camp walls, is forbidden...* Remember saying that? *And usually penalized by deportation. So don't do it because it's not worth it.* That was what you said. Don't you remember?' She doesn't recognize her own voice, is unsure whether she's pleading or begging or whether she's just angry. 'Besides, Poppy, we've got something to do now. Something worthwhile. We've got...' She waves at the books. 'We've got these.'

'It's not going to interfere with the library work, if that's what worries you. It's just mornings. Don't worry. Please.

I'm not. But…' She bites her lower lip. 'Don't tell. Promise. I don't want anyone, anyone else, to know about it. Not even Laurie. *Particularly* not Laurie. At this point. Not that he'd mind, of course. But anyway, he doesn't know. No one knows but you.'

'But what is it? What sort of job? And how did you find out about it?' Did she sit down opposite her? She thinks she did. She sees herself fetch a chair from the other side of the room, position it opposite her friend and slowly, very slowly – as if she's aged fast-forward during that short walk – sit so they are level with each other. Her voice calmer. 'Poppy, for heaven's sake. Is it legal? You're not really allowed, are you? Penalties. All sorts of problems. And Rufus? What on earth are you going to do with Rufus? For one thing.' How far can she go before she snaps the delicate thread that links their friendship?

Soft patches of pink show above the scarf at Poppy's throat, but the light has returned to her eyes and her gaze is level and clear.

'The teacher I've been nagging about for so long arrived the other day. He'll have about eight kids of various ages to school. Ruf will be one of them.' She brushes the desk in front of her with her hands.

'As for the job. It's only clerical. Just typing, filing and so forth. No big deal and working mornings only. Not very exciting really. But I have to do it.' She leans forward, her hands twisting.

'Dana. Listen. Listen to me. After I've done – everything I can possibly think of doing in the house. Once I've dressed and fed Rufus and read him a story, once I've hoovered up every last grain of sand, cleaned the wretched stove, wiped out the oven, shaken the toaster, polished the bath taps, thought through what we're having for lunch, for the evening meal – then, and only then, I work on the camp things. But once the committees are up and running, it's surprising how little time things actually take to keep moving. I read to Ruf again. We go outside for a walk. Then I sit down with a book while he plays at my feet. Any book. It doesn't much matter because for some reason I can't settle to read it. The other day I sat looking at a fly on my window. For a very long time. Do you know that if you listen hard enough the feet of a fly actually make a squeaky noise on the glass? Louder, much louder, than chalk on a blackboard. At first I was cross because I thought that if it marked the glass, I'd have to clean it. Then I realized that it would fill in another half an hour quite nicely, cleaning the bloody window. So it gleamed. So I could see it gleaming and enjoy the gleaming of it for another half an hour.' She looks down, bites her lip again. 'My freezer is full of meals packaged, marked and dated. It's neat. Our clothes are ironed and put away and all Laurie's socks match. Ruf's room is so neat you'd never know a little boy lived there. By each July I've written my Christmas cards and I'm the best pen pal you can imagine. Everything's all right. Really it is. Just that I need something to focus on. Before the…baby, before I lost the baby, it was more than all right. It was, almost, fine. It's just that now, for the moment, I need something else. Something to take my mind off things. Do you see? However elementary.' She stretches out her hand. 'I'm sorry, Dana. I shouldn't have put all this onto you. Just forget I mentioned it. Please.'

It is something like this she says, but what Dana thinks she hears is something altogether more violent. She remembers Poppy gave a shrug and a 'that's all there is to it' shake of her head. She remembers she wanted to say more, to beg her again to reconsider. But of course she doesn't. Her friendship with Poppy is too valuable to put on the line, so she enters into the agreement.

The little pile of books she was about to shelve rests on the crude table between them. As she picks them up she touches Poppy's hand.

'Of course I won't say anything,' she says, standing. 'But why are we doing this, Poppy? For Christ's sake. Why are we here? What are we doing here? You and me and the others who would rather be somewhere else? Who would rather be back where we were? If we were totally honest with ourselves, with each other – and with our husbands. Why are we here in this unreal place? Is it only the money? Is all this change of pace, this total change of lifestyle, this leaving behind of our family and friends, our jobs, our houses and pets, some of the older children who have to go back home to boarding schools – is it all in the name of money? And will it be worth it? Do you think? At the end of the day when the money's been spent, will it be worth it? Or it is something more that brings us here, keeps us here? Is it something else entirely? Please tell me it's more than pieces of silver.'

'That's easy to answer,' says Poppy. 'At least for us with children. That why I'm here. To keep the family together. To give Rufus a father. But you, for those of you without kids? If, as you say, you don't want to be here, then why are you? That I don't know.'

Dana hesitates. 'I'm here because of Dekker. And because I want a child; I want Dekker's child and living half a world away from each other was not a very smart way to solve that. But things are going wrong and I wonder what's happening to the person I was such a short time ago. It's just that when I look around at the number of people who came for three months and then stay on for three years or more, I get frightened. I don't want that to happen to me and I fear that the longer we're here, the harder it will be to function back in the real world. Everything's done for us on this camp. Washing machine dies, we call the maintenance man. Want something like this' – she taps the table –'you know someone who can knock one up. Need a dentist, we go across to the Dutch camp. It's parties every night, bridge or tennis or coffee or gym somewhere on camp every morning or afternoon. No bills, nothing to worry about, no money changing hands. Even down at the village shop, if you don't have enough cash, the man behind the till waves his hands, says pay next time. But no one ever does.

'It's dull and predictable and so safe that we're trapped. But we don't really mind after a while because we're fed and watered and treated quite well on the whole even if we're restricted on where we go and what we do – on pain of deportation. Or worse.' She shudders. 'You know, even after only just a few months, I have to pinch myself to think of the person I was before I got on that plane. I even wonder whether I could do now what I did then? I don't even *feel* like the same person. There's a set of expectations here and we – I – just fall in line.'

She glances down at the books in her hand. 'I had a father who expected things of me that I was unable to do. While I was working in an environment I loved, I was free of all those expectations. But you know something? I think I've stepped right back into line.'

She walks across the room, files the books under Mc and Mac until she sees she's shelved them back to front. Wrenches them out and reverses the sequence, wonders finally whether she's got it right. This is a different person from three months, six months ago. She will talk it through with Dekker. She doesn't recognize herself and she could do with guidance right now.

'Who am I?' she asks Dekker that evening.

'What do you mean, who are you?' He rests his copy of the latest issue of *Concrete Solutions* on his knee.

'I've lost me. The woman I spent the last eight years creating. I don't know whether I've died. Or gone awol. Or whether I'm just on holiday from being me. Would you like to come for a walk? We could walk out through the damned gates. There's a moon out tonight and it could look quite dramatic.'

'I've got enough drama on my hands on site at the moment.' He flicks the magazine irritably. 'Don't be fanciful. Your only trouble is that you think too much. Such men are dangerous.' He flaps the page.

'And women? What about women? Can thinking-too-much women be dangerous too?'

'Get a handle on it, Dana.' His frown deepens. Again he rustles the magazine, moves his feet. For the second time that week, he says, 'I'm not sure this conversation is going anywhere.'

He's right. It doesn't. She wonders at the wedge she can see opening between them, of which he seems either unaware or uncaring. Is it being here that's caused it or, as he said a few weeks back, was it always going to happen?

She pours herself another glass of apple juice. Clips the ceramic stopper hard over the bottle. She wants to talk. Knows she should ask him what it is that's causing the problem on site. She looks up ready to speak, but his brows are still knitted. He appears to be engrossed in what he is reading and she knows that to probe will only irritate him further. Or she could go for a walk by herself in the moonlight, a stroll around the inside perimeter of the wall.

He doesn't appear to notice when she rises and wanders into the dining room. Stands on a chair to lift the canvas from the top of the drinks dresser and when she finds it's no longer there, sits on the chair instead. She must have stored it in the bedroom wardrobe – not too many places a sizable canvas can be stored in this house. It's easy enough to check, but something stops her. She wonders at the urge that caused her to reach for the frustrating canvas anyway, her pad is filling so readily with drawings. She sits staring out across the rectangles of houses long after Dekker has gone to bed, until the shadows cast by the moon start to lengthen. She sits there so long that she thinks she sees someone crossing the sand, a lone figure moving across the camp in the moonlight. There one moment, gone the next. Being fanciful again, are you Dana?

Do you know, she hears Poppy say again, do you know you can hear a fly walking across a pane of glass? It's loud, louder than chalk on a blackboard. Louder than the crunch of a sandshoe on the shifting sand.

Although he had a name that wouldn't be out of place in Dickens, Edwin Priddle, the man hired to teach the younger kids on camp, was really quite unschoolteacherly.

Because there wasn't a lot that happened day-to-day on the site, the arrival of the headmaster, as he preferred to call himself, caused quite a commotion.

'Do you think he's for real? Edwin Priddle! How about that?'

'It could be an assumed name.'

'Why don't you women just give the chap a chance?'

'We are. Oh, we are.'

And they did. Even those who didn't have children went out of their way to make him feel as if he hadn't left the metropolis to come to this walled camp. They spoiled him and feted him because he had come. Which meant that the children could now, after all, enter into something resembling school life. Which meant that the mothers had even more time to do good works, to paint or write or read and keep house.

They took it in turns to invite him to dinner. The night they had him over, Dana made pumpkin soup followed by buttery rice served with a heap of spicy prawns bought freshly caught from down the coast that morning. It was still cool enough in the evenings, she thought, to close the meal with a hot syrup pudding, ice cream and strong coffee.

He didn't smoke and didn't drink which was unusual, but commendable, she thought in a teacher. Or a principal. But beyond that he was less categorical. He was vague about where he had come from and how long he would stay. Perhaps he was only being cautious. He had studied at Oxford, he said, and perhaps the silk cravat and waistcoat were a hangover from his student days. Even so, he seemed in some respect to be out of time. Unlike the other single men, he was housed in one half of a family house, the other half of which Poppy had negotiated for the library. So, Dana thought, in a way, he was really out of place, too.

NINETEEN

Taylor drops by the library when she's there on her own one morning.

'Another book for you. Or for the collection if you don't fancy it. And an invitation to bridge again on the Dutch camp. If you've a mind to join me.'

'Partner away again?' She is unable to hide the flash of sarcasm in her tone. Or perhaps she doesn't want to. Perhaps it's a relief to speak without thinking. A release of some sort. She rarely, she realizes, talks to Dekker like that.

He sticks his tongue in his cheek.

'Something like that. Think on it anyway.' And he's off across the sand before she has time to ask him when.

After dinner Dekker is busy brewing. It's not her evening in the library and she walks back and forth between lounge and bedroom trying to convince herself it's not too early to go to bed. She picks up her book and puts it down. Starts to write a letter to her parents and gives up.

In the kitchen, a dozen apple juice bottles lined up on the metal draining board beside the sink, Dekker gently levering a teaspoon of sugar into each. She leans against the table to watch him. 'What's the sugar for?'

'It primes the brew. Makes more fizz essentially.'

'Dekker. I've been thinking… Why don't we have bridge here? Just one night a week, say, or even every couple of weeks. Make a change, give us something to centre our minds on.'

He looks around briefly, nods. 'But why bridge, eh? Why not darts or…well a slide evening even. Something like that?'

'Well, yes. I just thought that something that could, you know, form a bit of a structure would be good. Something regular. Exercise our minds.'

'I've got plenty to exercise my mind right now.' He sighs, places a cap on one of the bottles and seals it. 'Two of the draftsmen quit today. Just like that.' He clicks his fingers. 'Now we have to train up someone else. And one of the dredgers has fouled…' He stares at the bottle-top sealer.

'Will you have to bring them in from overseas? The men I mean.'

'Yes, yes, of course. No one here with the experience. Besides as you know I don't like cards…'

'I never think of bridge as cards…'

'No you don't. I know you don't. But it is. Nevertheless. Besides you play anyway at the Dutch camp.'

'Yes. But that's only every so often. Now and again as a fill-in. Just to make up a table.'

'Look,' he says. 'I'd really rather not. I know very little about the game and it's not something that interests me. But there's nothing to stop you. Why don't you go ahead?'

'That's not the point. Exactly. I thought it was something we could do together?'

Does she say that or just think it and does it matter anyway, she asks herself. Part of her knows that it does matter. But in the end it is too easy to slip out into the dark for a walk around the edge of the camp, to end up at the door of the metal transportable.

'Thought you'd come,' he says as he opens it.

'Are you saying I'm predictable?'

He doesn't bother to answer. Instead spins the top off a bottle of Glenfiddich, sends a splash of the liquid spinning into the bottom of a thick tumbler.

'Here.' He half-fills the glass with tap water and pops the drink into her hand. 'Since you like the stuff so much.'

'I do. I do actually. Compared to apple juice. Or that ghastly home-brew they call wine.' She seats herself on the carpet. Cross-legged with her back against the other chair. 'You asked me for bridge, but didn't say when.'

'Uh, so that's why you're here. You didn't look that interested. So there didn't seem much point pursuin' it.' He looks at her sharply. 'How's the paintin' coming along then?'

She looks away.

'I'm not sure that it is. I had the start of something, but it was hardly a painting. A portrait I'd started. It sounds silly, but in ash…'

'And?'

'And, well nothing really. Last time I looked it wasn't where I left it and I haven't had the heart to search for it. If

I'm honest, I'm trying to paint because I feel I *should* be able to, that surely it can't be that hard... And to be more honest still...I'm not really sure I've the talent for it, never mind the skill.'

'P'raps you're being too hard on y'self.'

Perhaps I am, she wants to say. She wants to say more because she senses he will look underneath her words to what she is unable to express and in that way know more about her. She needs to tell him that she finds it easier to draw than to paint, that the pictures unfold from her mind quite naturally that way. But she is unable to explain to herself why it should matter what he thinks or why it matters. Then, too, she can't be sure of him. Of how he would react if she said something like: But don't you see, I have to be hard on myself. I have to have some focus, something other than Dekker, other than me. I feel like a seed sealed into a slip of silver paper with lots of like seeds for company, but no light, no warmth, no sustenance. Waiting for the dark to open up. She wants to say this or something like it, but she fears that as receptive as he appears to be on the surface, this sort of sentiment would test his patience. She remembers the first time she met him when he sat at her kitchen table with the half-eaten sandwich in both hands, remembers the laughter that blocked her out, that joined the two men. Wonders, then, whether he would understand what she was saying any more than her husband. Whether he would care.

'Sometimes that's all you have to do,' he's saying. 'Set the needle on the plastic. Oft'n times, it's the only way you can set the music free.'

She holds her glass up towards the dim bulb swinging softly from the ceiling above. Squints through the liquid to arrest the sudden exposure she feels…at what? Because he listened? Or is it because there's something like kindness in his tone? When she brings the malt slowly to her lips, the dryness of it catches at the edges of her tongue, the roof of her mouth. She sucks into the flavor. 'Aren't you going to have something? Something to drink?'

'Don't feel the need. Currently.'

'Is there anything you have the need for? Didn't I ask you that once before?' Her tone deceptively light.

'Whoa there.' He whistles gently. 'You are on the warpath tonight. What's up?'

'I just wonder when you're going to seduce me, that's all.'

'Bit sudden, isn't?' And then when she shrugs, 'That's entirely up to you.'

'Up to me?' Her laugh is hard-edged. 'Forgive me, but I thought it took two?'

'It's a decision you have to make. Not me.'

'Why? Why me? Why not you? Have you already decided?'

'I'm a man, aren't I? I'm surprised you even have to ask.'

She hears voices outside, the banging of one of the doors down the way, a child's cry. Inside the cabin, not even a clock ticks. Much more of this and I, too, will be hearing flies walk up walls, scorpions across sand.

'Well?' Her invitation hangs for long minutes in the softly lit room, takes off in little echoes that bounce from wall to wall until they disappear entirely, dying somewhere they can do no harm. The sounds outside recede, too, until all she can hear is her own breath, until it seems it's no longer dark here in his palace, but light as day. Until there is nothing between them but air.

'Bridge then. Saturd'y 5 o'clock if you can make it. I'll pick you up a bit before that.' He gets up, stretches slowly and deliberately, muscle by muscle, a dog's first movement of the morning.

It is then that the anger that has been shifting about in her all day, no, longer than that, for days, ever since Poppy's announcement and perhaps before that too, shoots through her. Anger – or was it panic – at the thought of the lonely evening ahead. She scrambles to her feet, sets down the glass with the liquid barely tasted, swings to face him.

'Are you turning me down?' She hears her own voice, crisp as a dry biscuit.

'Is that what it looks like?' I'm just giving you the time to think things through. To make a decision you're not going to regret.' His tone is measured, almost mild.

He moves purposefully towards the door.

That is all it takes for her to do what she later realizes was inevitable all along. She knows, too, in this same instant, that her mind is as keen as it ever was. That the shadow crossing the sand the other night was real. Not a ghost. Not a creature freed from deep inside a mind intent on its own escape, but a person. A real live person walking through the camp in the early morning. That the canvas, too, should have been where she left it. And that it has been removed. That she has been wrong to doubt her mind.

Afterwards she navigates the sparseness of the small kitchen to make two mugs of tea. Thinking as she moves around that this is all you need really, this size space, these implements, all this is quite adequate. There is something liberating in working naked in the kitchen of someone she knows so little of. Of someone I *expect* little of, she tells herself. The water boils quickly in the thin saucepan and again the water sizzles and spits up the sides of the pan like a surprised kitten.

'As a matter of interest,' she says as she carries the mugs around the flimsy partition to the bed. 'Since you know so much about the lore of the land, as a matter of interest, what's the penalty for adultery here?' She sets the drinks down, sits on the edge of the bed.

'For a man? A fine. Ten riyals, perhaps. Maybe less. For a woman? Stoning. Death.' He lies flat on his back staring across at her, his arms folded behind his head.

She doesn't quite know how she feels as she walks back in through her own front door. Only that her head is high with something that could be defiance or pride and that her back is straighter than it has been for some time. She tells herself that she is an adulteress, that she has broken heaven knows how many laws as well as the seventh commandment. She tells herself that she should feel guilty. But dig as she might, the feeling of letting Dekker down won't surface.

All the same, the short sharp click the latch makes as it engages and again as the door closes behind her sounds louder than usual. Dekker glances up from whatever he was reading and she can tell from the look on his face that he hasn't known she has been out. She smiles at him and goes through to the other room. Back here it's just the same as it was an hour ago. Is that all it was? Just one hour? An hour she thinks she would gladly trade to have her life back where it was before. Dekker, herself, her job, his parents and hers on the end of the line, all the little scoops and spoonfuls that made up her life. Like a cutlery canteen with the shapes and depressions stamped out of the smooth green baize so that they all slot back in so readily it doesn't take thought. A comfy cocoon, her friend had called it. *The world is not about to end because you get out of your comfy cocoon.* A big piece of my world has, Margot.

She showers, goes to bed. Flicks off the bedside lamp and allows herself to think backwards. Because you can try to erase back home. You can endlessly try, and you can adjust to not having it, but you can't wipe it out as if it never existed. And back home right now the tenants in their apartment will have six months of their lease still to run. Down in Constantia, Dekker's parents will be walking their ridgebacks Chakka and Tiwi through the thick bush, his mother carrying the snake kit with the sharp knife, the permanganate of potash and the tourniquet in the little white pouch with the red cross on the flap. Breaths of wind will wriggle loose the last leaves of the grape vines so they fall to lie in drifts of crispy yellows and browns and oranges, so Elisha, the Xhosa maid, will moan and mutter as she picks up the straw brush to sweep the arcades yet again. Back home, too, in the home before the one she shared with Dekker well before the last uncertain days of Southern Rhodesia, the silver-green branches of her father's olive trees will sag untidily under the weight of purplish-black fruit the size of small plums. And each time he walks past, Peter Novotny will show his pride in them by threatening to harvest. She sees him smiling. Shaking his fist. And the museum? Do they still talk of her? Or is she just one more exhibit whose time has come and gone.

And now what have I done? A cold dead feeling in her chest. Her body rigid. She pulls the sheet up over her eyes.

TWENTY

The next morning, she tells herself nothing's changed, that the sex has changed nothing, but there is a part of her that knows this is not so, and that her relationship with Taylor has expanded beyond the neat box she put it in. Although she tries to suppress it, there is the uncomfortable knowledge that although she may still regard Taylor as her mentor and nothing more, it is her opinion of herself that has altered. Moving from lounge to bedroom was too easy altogether and she is a little scared of the side to her character she sees emerging. A latent schizophrenia perhaps that she can be one person all her life until now, is still that person one moment, but with the capacity to be totally different the next. Until she steps back into the first person and then it is unthinkable she could be unfaithful. The word itself makes her feel slightly sick.

She is about to slide back the door to go out into the garden she has come to think of as her own Arabian oasis, when something causes her to glance upwards to where her canvas had been stashed on top of the dresser. She blinks to see it back there again. Just as it was before. With the edge projecting slightly over the edge. She steps up onto a chair, looks at it carefully. No change, just as it was before. The start of a drawing of a woman who, with her long straight hair, a cigarette held loosely between her fingers, is clearly Anna. Why it is now back where it was or why it went missing in the first place, she is unable to fathom. Only Dekker could have removed it and there would be no reason for him to do so. Or if he did, no reason to put it back. No one else has been in here. He might have been showing it to someone. To Anna herself? Or showing it off as pride in his wife's work perhaps? Then again. Maybe it never moved.

She gets down, moves past the wall of heat that's building up against the glass, steps out into the little garden, slides the door closed to keep in the cool. The shrubs have recovered surprisingly quickly from their battering, put on both height and girth since the *shamal*, the leafy tops branching and shooting almost level with her head. It no longer looks like a palisade of stakes, but it is her fortress nonetheless. The sun is still low enough to work; she turns to fetch her sketchbook and then on a whim decides to fetch the easel and work on the canvas for a change. Now that it has reappeared. Although the promised patio has yet to be laid and there are no bricks or concrete on which to set the easel, she digs the legs into the sand, turns the structure towards the east. It's early still so she has time to work before the light changes. She wants the canvas free of shadow save those already set in the lines that are emerging in the portrait. She wants the golden light of the earlier part of the day. Before the sun steals the colour from the morning.

She sets the board on the easel, studies the drawing with an almost clinical intent and searches for the anger that caused her to toss the canvas on top of the cupboard. A month ago? Two months? At least double that time. Wonders how it is that such a level of fury can dissolve. Has it really dissipated? Or is it waiting for her? One thing is for sure: it is not here, in this drawing. In this action of moving the work towards completion.

The outline of the face is more or less right, she thinks, with the shading in the lower cheeks bringing the bone structure to life, and the angle of the head – the slight tilt as her face is lifted for another pull at her cigarette – emphasizing a hardness about the lips and chin. But it is the empty sockets of the eyes she needs to work on. She has a mind to try to represent the distraction she saw in them when she first met Anna. But the other times their paths have crossed, when Anna has been in company, sometimes Dekker's company, the light they emit has been quite different.

It is then she remembers the sketch she was working on the day Anna asked for a lift. She goes indoors to fetch the pad, flips through it until she comes to the profile of the face, wonders what it is about Anna that has caused her to start drawing her twice now. As if the suppressed antipathy she senses between them draws her in like a Siamese cat. But here, on the sketchpad, the eyes are alive: her long, narrow eyes are wide on this page. With surprise, horror, wonder? She cannot remember what had been in her mind when she drew them like this. But then what she sees or reads into this representation, another person may not. Interpretation. Isn't that part of the wonder of art, any art? In the sketch, the face is puffy in parts, too, as if she has been crying, and the mouth not as full as it is on the canvas. The cigarette in one hand, yes, but the other bent to support the chin. For the first time she is absorbed, conscious but uncaring of figures walking past.

The sun is way up by the time she steps to one side, stretches her back and presses her hands into her spine to ease it. She collapses the easel, places the painting back on top of the dresser, slips the crayons back into the box, and starts towards the kitchen to make lunch. Finds herself thinking of Taylor, of how little she knows of his life, pushes the thoughts aside. At least the portrait distracted her. And after lunch she might call on Poppy. Although they share the library work, in taking turns to open it on alternate days and leaving their questions and answers for each other on the small pad, they rarely see each other and she is anxious to learn how the job is going.

It's only when she calls around later that afternoon and notices the sand piling up once again on the front porch that she realizes that some time has elapsed since she's been here, remembers the time they sat on that step talking after the *shamal* and the relief she felt that the turmoil in Poppy's life was starting to settle back down, the relief a release, like the click of a padlock springing open. Then chides herself for noticing such a housekeeperly and completely unimportant detail as piled-up sand. How about getting stuck into your own housekeeping before you judge others, she is saying to herself as the door swings open and Poppy is there, larger than life as usual, wearing her favourite brown skirt with the soft blue scarf wound around her neck and trailing down her back. But even so, as Dana's gaze travels on into the house despite her efforts to keep her eyes level, she can't help noticing that Poppy's house, Poppy's perfect house, is full of sand. She flushes, raises her eyes instantly, but Poppy has seen her glance; Poppy knows without looking how her house is.

'Oh yes,' she says, biting her lip and arching one eyebrow. 'I know. Bad, isn't it? I…I haven't really had time. What with one thing and another.' She looks about herself quickly, puts her hand to her throat fingering her scarf. Pulls the cloth a little higher. 'Tea? Coming in for a cuppa? Or something stronger?'

'Lovely. But only if you have time. I feel bad.' I feel bad she wants to say for not coming around sooner on the one hand and now for taking up your time when you don't have time to spare. Bad on both counts. Oh, to have a telephone. There has been talk of telephone connections, but just when that will be no one knows. The air in the house is thick. No, not thick, she corrects herself, rather more than that: edgy, uncertain, short on oxygen. As if the wind is blowing still. Or as if there's a storm on the way, somewhere out of sight, but closing in. She tries to keep her voice light as she follows her friend into the kitchen. 'How's it going? The job? Ruf at school? Everything?'

Poppy doesn't answer at first. She keeps her eyes on the kettle she's holding under the tap. Fills it carefully through the spout. Places it on the bench and plugs it in. She unhooks two mugs from where they hang under the top cupboard. Each movement she makes is separate from the last as if she is receiving instructions from another source. She turns to face Dana.

'The job's gone.'

'Gone?' Dana frowns, shakes her head. 'How? I mean, why?'

'Embarrassing really. Yes, embarrassing is what it is. Mainly. That's all.' She sucks in her cheeks, standing with her fingers looped through the handles of the mugs while the kettle fumes behind her. 'What's to tell?' She shrugs, her eyes turned up towards the ceiling. Her lips twist and she lifts her shoulders a second time.

'Nothing really. There was a raid. The other day. I suppose I could have seen it coming, but I didn't. None so blind, they say. Anyway, they came, the *mutaween* – the police – to take me back home. They were…polite enough, not rough, not really rough. It's just it was… humiliating, I suppose that's it. More than anything else. But a bit frightening too. They brought me here, brought me home. We waited for Laurie. And then.' She breathes deeply. 'Then they got him to sign a form to say, to swear, that he would never let me work here, work in Saudi, again.' She turns away, stares at the kettle as it continues to boil. 'Laurie was, is, understandably angry. Of course. Naturally. It reflects on him, you see. What he lets his wife get up to.' She sets one of the mugs down on the counter with some force, grips the other hard in both hands and stares into it as if it contains a potion that will change everything back the way it was. Without taking her gaze from the inside of the cup, she swings back towards Dana.

'I shouldn't have done it, Dana. I know I shouldn't have done it. *I* knew that. *You* knew. You tried to stop me. Everyone who comes here knows the system. I knew what the law was when I came here. But I wouldn't listen, would I? I broke the law. And that we've been here way, way longer than I ever dreamed is no excuse. I'm not stupid. I knew what I was doing. Some part of me took over and just railroaded my rational self and at the time what I had to do seemed quite clear. But that is no excuse; there is no excuse you see. Do you hear me...' She is shouting now. 'No excuse. I shouldn't have been working. I should have been satisfied with what I have. I should have been satisfied I've got everything, simply everything...' The handle of the mug snaps off. A cut across her palm she doesn't notice. 'The worst part of the whole thing, the absolutely worst part, is that Laurie trusted me. After all, after everything, he still trusted me. And now...' Her voice breaks.

Dana swings her around to the sink, places her hand under the tap, lets the water run. She keeps her own voice to a murmur, hugs Poppy's shaking shoulders. You did it for the best. It's okay. No harm's been done. Poppy, no harm's been done. It'll be okay. You know it will.' Over and over, she says the same thing. But now she is close, now her head is so close to Poppy's, she wonders whether it will be all right. Around Poppy's wrist, just below the seeping palm is a ring of blue. And when she looks closer, about her neck, imperfectly hidden by the scarf is another ring, thicker, a smudgy purplish-blue. Below that, another, yellowing.

Oh Poppy,' she whispers. She keeps her arm about her shoulders as they stand at the kitchen sink. She rocks her slightly. The view out through the window is sand. And beyond that? The wall. Grey against the white-hot sky. Oh Poppy, keep clear the path to your front door.

TWENTY-ONE

Her visits to the cabin become more frequent. It's inevitable she tells herself. Most times she talks for the term of her visit and she might leave after ten minutes or after an hour or more with a book. Or a thought. Sometimes they move to his bed. Strangely one is part of the other. It is her own words that sound in her ears afterwards. He listens, watches. Like a cobra, eyes unmoving, lidded, alert. When she steps down from the transportable she doesn't care about the eyes that might be watching from behind curtained windows. Or the fact that it is early or late or that the heat is rising so strongly from the sand that it makes the row of houses opposite swim in the air. The guilt for her is that afterwards she feels so free.

All the same, it's there, the uncomfortable knowledge of what she is doing. One afternoon she asks what exactly comprises adultery in terms of Saudi law. 'I mean, well, given that the punishment so savage – and for the female, final – I imagine they'd have to be pretty sure. Or would they? But how would they know without, well – without examining? And even then? How can they tell for sure?'

She carries in the metal teapot, two mugs, sets them down on the bedside table, vaults lightly on top of him. She likes the way his belly wobbles when she makes him laugh as he does now, likes the ease of their naked bodies with each other. Likes the ease.

'They figure out whether it's punishable or not if they are able to pass a string between the couple,' he says. 'And,' he adds, 'if they're acting on a tip-off, you'd better believe they're not too fussy whether or not they get it right.'

She grimaces. 'And then what? They lie there meekly, still coupled I suppose? Until it's proven. I don't believe it!'

He laughs. 'You look like Lady Godiva sitting up there,' he says. His head tilted back, looking up at her.

'I'm not sure I like that.'

'Like what?'

'The comparison.'

'Uh.'

'Well, wasn't she a prostitute?'

'You're the one making the connection. That's not the way the story comes to me. Rather the opposite. She was a one-woman union the way I read it. Paraded herself starkers through the streets in an effort to stop the unfair taxes her hubbie levied on the good citizens of the town.'

'I'm afraid I don't get any sort of connection.' She leans backwards, puzzled.

'Literal. Aren't you? I wasn't looking for the third degree. Just taken in by your long hair for a moment. The length of it. And the way it falls, I suppose. And your necklace.' He reaches up, gently brushes a lock from her breast and she is half-annoyed at her body's defiance of her conscious mind, the electricity that passes across the hollow of her belly. She moves, restless.

'My hair is yellow, too, I suppose? And any sort of music is totally missing from my make-up.' She glances down at her breast. 'And now I'm lopsided.'

'The music'll come. One day I suspect you'll find the music in you. Right now, you've got too much going on in your head. Too much forcing happenin'. Music's something you have to have space for. Like the paintin'. But if you come down here and lie beside me for a moment, I think I can fix the lopsidedness for you'

For a few seconds she thinks of resisting and then there's something in the set of his mouth that draws her down.

But mostly they talk. Or she talks and he listens. It has become a routine, a comfortable routine. When she arrives, depending on the time of day or night, he will either flick the switch for the kettle or spin the top from a bottle of Scotch as deftly as he flicks the cards. A moment is all it takes, a moment of adjustment between one state of being and another, a threshold that divides what has gone before from what is about to happen or what might happen, an instant of grace that allows each to gauge the appetite or the mood of the other. Sometimes she sits on the other less comfortable chair. Or she may settle on the carpet to lean against his knee. Or pace from one side of the short space to the other. She may talk for an hour. Or two. At first she talks mainly about her work, about the friends they had in Johannesburg, about wanting children as much as Dekker, but after Poppy's experience not wanting to conceive here. She watches him for signs of boredom. Surely his lids are so low he must be asleep? Waits for him to yawn or wriggle his toes, shift about in his chair, but he watches her, unmoving, his body still, his eyes under the half-closed lids following her gestures, her movements. As if he's interested. In her and in what she's saying.

You don't need to knock, he has told her. Day or night, my door is always open for you. If I'm not home, and if you have a mind to, come in and wait for me. Still she has determined that she will always knock; her own tradition is too strong for this not to happen. To enter the metal van in his absence is one of the two boundaries between them over which she will not step.

A dilemma is arising between her and Dekker as to where they should settle when they leave the Middle East. The most obvious place is Johannesburg. She would like nothing better than to return to Johannesburg and her old job. Well? He shrugs. But Dekker sees more future for us in Sydney. There are pluses and minuses to both places, she says. And if we return to Johannesburg, we're still miles from my parents who are in Southern Rhodesia. And his too, who live in the Cape. Just as far away. I think it's something that we're all going to have to live with. That our respective families are never going to be geographically close.

'Positives and negatives to that. Positives and negatives to most things I've come across,' he says.

Her husband's parents live in Constantia, she tells him. In a large house made even grander by the Dutch gables, the vine-covered arcades, the olive groves that surround it. His mother manages it, she says, manages it with just one maid, a Xhosa woman. As she paces about the room, she demonstrates Xhosa for him, the small amount she has absorbed, the clicks and balances of a language that some day she will take time to learn properly. They have dogs. Ridgebacks with coats as cool and slick as cobra skin and bodies with the speed to match. She talks more about her parents-in-law than about her own mother and father. I'm closer to Dekker's parents. Particularly his mother. Why is that? He asks. Why?

She shrugs. Even to Taylor she doesn't want to admit she finds it difficult to talk to her own. To confess that even though they live closer than Dekker's parents it's easier not to visit them with their unspoken expectations just under the surface of every meeting. What would they think of her right now? Sprawled on the carpet in her lover's lounge while her husband sits at home with his engineering manuals? With her attempts to paint or draw just as abortive here as they were there? She looks down to pull a loose thread from the sleeve of her blouse. It's a yellow gypsy blouse with a low neck she has chosen to wear today and for a moment she is distracted. Thinks how well the egg-yolk yellow goes with the crisp whiteness of the skirt.

She doesn't know how to answer him. His question disturbs her and in doing so frees up something inside her to ask him a question of her own, totally unrelated to his, and dangerously close to their unspoken no-go zone. She knows already what his reaction will be and in some part of herself she knows it's something that should remain just where it is. That she shouldn't prod or tamper, that it is no business of hers and that it will threaten something she has begun to value. She knows that this is a part of Taylor's life that belongs to solely to Taylor and that while he shares everything else with her, this he will not share. But recently it is something that has begun to nibble at her mind, her mind that was a master at making Shakespeare's *heaven out of hell and hell out of heaven* one of her realities. And now it won't be held back any longer. It comes out in a rush of words and it's nothing at all, but something she's compelled to ask. She tells herself she will not know the answer until she asks the question, that it will batter itself to death in her mind until she hears it from him. Until it's no longer guesswork on her part, but something that can be discussed between them like everything else they talk about. She settles herself on the carpet, raises her head to meet his gaze.

'For the same reason – perhaps for the same reason – you say nothing about your home, about your wife. Don't you miss her? Do you miss your wife?'

The words drop quite casually into the space between them to settle on the slices of light the afternoon sun has angled through the slatted blinds onto the carpet. She's sitting across from him, on a cushion on the floor, and it is late afternoon – almost time for her to return home to put on the kettle for Dekker's tea – when the words are out, ranged across the space between them. It occurs to her, too late, that her raising of the subject just at this moment when it is nearly time to leave is provoked by time running out between them. That is all she can think as she waits for him to reply. But in answer he says nothing. Continues to gaze across at her, over the words sticking up between them like the colourful letters of children's alphabet blocks and the only hint she gets that her question has hit its target is a small tightening of his lips. And a type of sadness, although not that exactly, that settles in the skin around his eyes. That asks, rather than warns, her to go no further.

'How's the paintin' comin' along then?'

Her eyes flash. 'You didn't answer my question,' she says shortly.

'No,' he agrees. 'But then you haven't answered mine.' And when she says nothing, he follows her gaze into the shafting light. 'Just seems a good idea to me to move things into safer waters…'

She's caught in a stickiness of her own making. Has made her way into her own web, a tangle where she's unreasonably glad she has hurt him. It's only when he continues speaking that she becomes aware she has been holding her breath.

'It's not important,' he adds. 'Some things are better left unsaid.'

'For me it's important,' she insists, then realizes with shock that this is the first time it has become important, this moment of saying it aloud. Like hot lava finding a crack in a crust of self-denial. She is aware of him watching her struggle to stem the flow, to mend this fissure that's suddenly opened in front of her, to push away the thought of a wife back home who enjoys him as she does herself and gives him more than she ever can, has the right to give him more – pies and puddings, children, grandchildren. Has had that rightful place for ever and a day. While she, Dana Novotny, an out-of-work adulteress, has traded all that for a fragment of a nameless woman's husband. A situation that even in this moment of panic, she knows she has brought squarely on herself. 'I don't…I don't even know, for instance,' she says lamely, backing off a little from the tension around his eyes, 'whether you have children.'

'Of course I do. I'm of an age, and from an era, when having children was not something you debated. Or thought through even. If you married, it was a given.' His eyelids droop and she knows him well enough to know that it is not because he is weary or bored; it is to hide his eyes, to keep his secrets safe, to drop a veil between one part of his life and the other. She wants to tell him that this very act gives away what he is trying to hide. And not to bother because she is getting to know him so well that she can paint in a picture without his words. Or wouldn't it be more truthful to admit that she wants him to say the words – the names of his wife and family, where they live, what they look like, what they do – so that once shared perhaps it will no longer be so threatening to her?

But in the reasoning that sits between one part of her mind and the other, she knows this is not the case, that he will never allow her to invade that particular space; she is aware, too, if she's honest that she doesn't know him, and following this attempt at honesty she feels a measure of relief as she suspects he is a man no woman will ever really know.

Later still, when she has time to reflect, she realises her attack was a reaction to his question about her parents and it's not that they were anything but good parents, she tells herself. They loved her and there was nothing they did that was wrong. But all the same she has trouble drawing a full breath when she thinks of them, a band around her ribcage.

The next time she sees him he tells her he has two boys, or that's how he still thinks of them, as boys, even though they're now grown with their own families. How old, she wants to know. Oh, late twenties, early thirties. Your age, not much different.'

'I wish I was older for you.' Her voice is wistful.

'Your age.' He shakes his head. 'That's part of the attraction,' he says drily.

TWENTY-TWO

In the mail Dekker brought home with him one evening there was a package containing a pile of shining brochures that now lie in a heap on the dining table.

'A holiday on a boat in Greece. And we're so close to the Greek islands here. What do you think. Just the ticket, eh?' They look through the pamphlets. She hasn't seen Dekker so enthusiastic in a long while and at first it is exciting comparing the quality of one pack of lies with the next – unpacking the truth from under the spin. Laughing together. And then one heap of bare rock starts to resemble the next until, pretty soon, she knows this is not where she wants to go. Besides, not only is she a poor sailor but she doesn't much like boats either, and nor, she had thought, did Dekker. In the past they had often discussed the reality behind the colour pictures of a cruise: that once you are on board, you can't get off until the craft docks. But she doesn't really want to go anywhere at the moment. Perhaps finally she has settled down enough to relax, to enjoy herself. In a way she hadn't imagined, is she doing that? Or is she afraid that if she leaves, even if it is only for a holiday, she will be unable to return. Or is it that Poppy needs her? And Taylor? How central is Taylor to her sudden reluctance to leave?

Dekker places his hand over hers. 'You don't look that keen. Eh?'

'Just…thinking it through a bit. I thought it was a trip to the Cape we were thinking of planning? To see your folks? This is – sudden, that's all. When were you thinking we might go?'

'October. Mid-to-late October.'

As always, he has it planned already. His hand is hot on hers and now the perspiration is starting to build between the two.

'And you? What do you want?'

Does he say that or does she imagine it? What do I want, she asks herself? I want my marriage back the way it was when we looked, really looked, at each other, different from what it's like with Taylor, but in its own way just as satisfying. When we laughed and talked and thought up names for the babies we were going to have. When we knew so much about each other's totally opposite careers that you once joked we could swap jobs for a day or a week and the output would be the same. But it doesn't happen like that, you've already told me that. I don't want to island-hop in Greece, gawk at dervishes in Turkey or clamber over ruins in Syria. I want to see more of here, more of Arabia than the local *suq*, than the road up to al-Dhuraf, more than the black-cloaked women, the *mutaween* with their canes. I want to do what Jane Digby did and ride through the desert on horseback. Or camel. Or goat. Or just go mad for want of love and understanding like Qays and draw my pictures, flimsy as life, in the sand. Like Poppy, I want something more than I have. I want more than a walled camp, full of same-same houses and furniture and crockery, more than rounds of parties, bridge, tennis and coffee. And yet – and yet two minutes ago I was happy with this. I didn't want to leave. I was happy here. That's what I said. That's what I thought. Wasn't it?

She shivers. It's as if she has swum from a warm sea into a cold current. She glances sideways at Dekker who is still looking at a picture of a rowing boat, painted in blue and white, red oars stowed. A beach, trees – olive trees perhaps – mountains in the distance. Over their breathing she hears the ticking of the clock on the wall opposite.

Heraclitus' river roaring by, rushing around me. I stand waist-deep in the tumbling waters as it surges by without even recognizing me. Not even an obstacle in its path.

She withdraws her hand from under his. Out loud she says. 'For me, right now, I'm okay. I don't mind it here. Actually.'

'And if you change your mind? It will be too late by then to book. October is the best month. When it's cooler.'

'You go. Why don't you go?'

TWENTY-THREE

It's August, the time of the year when people are leaving the camp, when others are coming in. The social pace is frenetic. She goes to three parties in the space of twenty-eight hours. She plays bridge five or six times a week. When she goes out to play tennis at eight o'clock in the morning, the humidity settles over her like a cloud and her clothes are plastered to her skin before she even gets to the court. There's another purge on women working – a timely reminder to the new batch coming in – one woman deported, the husbands of the others ordered to sign a document swearing their women will not work in Saudi Arabia again.

She is clear now what she wants from her friendship with Tay. It becomes easier and easier to drop into the metal cabin where she talks about things and emotions, about relevancies and irrelevancies, about jobs and painting, about love and affairs, all spilling from her like rice from a canister. The sex she places to one side. Rarely, if ever, does he either suggest or instigate it, neither does he turn her down when she moves towards him.

What is the most important thing in a relationship, she asks him. A genuine liking for one another, he replies. For me, she says, trust is the most important thing. He shrugs. We're all different. Main thing is to be true to yourself. You can't do better than that. Another time, he says: Problem with trust is that it's based on expectation. You trust somebody and lumber them with your set of rules at the same time.

The urge she had felt to find out more about him has left her. In place of her former curiosity, she is relieved she cannot envisage a past for him. She tells him this.

Good, he says. I'm relieved to hear it. Because all I have is right here, in front of you. There's nothing else. I've nothing to offer.

But still, she tempers. For all that. Surely it's the past that makes the present? Look at how when we meet people, we go out of our way to find out about where they've lived and where they've been. Doesn't the past mold you? The past with all your experiences? Make you the person you are?

Listen to yourself. You've talked your way in a circle back to where we started.

But what about me? What about what I've told you about my past?

What about it? Do you think it makes me see you any differently then? Treat you any different? Natural that the past has brought us to the present. But there's only point to the present – it's the only thing really relevant. Nothing else matters.

But he had told her once that he was born in London.

What part of London?

The south. From the Thames. I'm the man from the Thames. And when he said that, she witnessed the same pride in him as the first time she stepped up into his house. And it *does* make her see him differently – this pride in where he's from.

Sometimes they debate, other times she listens. But mainly she talks. There's no one alive, she thinks, who would listen so patiently, for so long. When she lies in bed at night, it's her own voice she hears reverberating. During the day, it's his phrases that arrive in her head. She wonders aloud one day whether he's gathering material for a novel.

'Either that, or you're a frustrated psychoanalyst.'

He laughs. 'Writin' a book like all the rest, you mean? Yeah, oft'n thought about it. But. Like the rest, there's a chasm between the thinkin' and the doin'. Not sure I'm cut out for it.'

'They were saying. The other night they were saying that life gets greyer as you get older and that this is a sign of maturity. What do you think?'

'It's the compromise in getting old they're on about.' He shrugs. 'Not something I bother to think about.'

'For me, life is becoming clearer as time goes on, definite outlines of black and white. Compromise is a very dull way to think of things, anyway. If there has to be some sort of middle ground, I much prefer to think of it as balance.'

'Rare to find balance, rarer still to be able to hang onto it. As for black and white, never think that way m'self. In a manner of speakin', it's been my experience that there's always a bit of one mixed in with the other. A bit of push and pull.

She remembers her wish to swim in the clear green waters of the Gulf and she asks him to take her to the sea.

'To swim,' she says. 'Not a seaside village like Qatif, but somewhere I can swim.' Perhaps after bridge one night?'

'Morning's the best. Early morning. If you're up to it.'

It's several days later with the camp still in darkness when he turns out of the gates to drive her down the coastal highway and they haven't gone far when he turns off quite suddenly onto an invisible track and switches off the motor.

'Not overly keen on getting bogged down. Under the circs. We'll walk. Not far, just over that rise there.'

'The sea, this close? I had no idea it was so near. If I had known, I could have walked here.' She follows quickly, lengthening her stride to place her footsteps in his and shortly there's the sea, not the translucent green she has held in her memory, but darker in the pre-dawn, small waves washing up onto a smooth beach. He is stepping out of his shorts as she turns to him, her eyes full. 'And seagulls. So long since I've seen a bird…'

'Get your gear off then. We'll have a bit of a swim and bob along out there with them. We don't have all that long…' He drops his watch on top of his clothes, wades into the foaming breakers and launches himself into a comfortable crawl out to where the water swells gently, flips over onto his back and floats.

Other things suddenly more important than swimming. The way the light is changing, the pale peach wash of the sky, the colour that's arriving in the day. The gulls are playing tag, challenging each other, swooping in and out of the short waves that collapse in frothy lines one on top of the other. The tide is going out, the sand at her feet shines like silk in the rising sun, captures the length of her shadow stretching back in the direction of the camp; behind her feet her reflection lies in a puddle. It's on firm sand like this that Qays would have written his verses. On wet hard sand where it will last until the next full tide. She slips off her sandals. Just wants to walk. Knows the sand in the glass is running out.

Not long after, he catches up with her, and they drop together on the beach. When he makes love to her, his body is cold against hers, his mouth tastes of salt.

'Was floatin' out there one day, my mind somewhere else, when I felt a tickle on my leg,' he says in the car going back. 'Raised my head a bit to see a sea snake twinin' itself around my ankle.'

'Ugh. What did you do? Are they poisonous?'

'Flung it off, flipped over and swam like mad for shore. And, yes, very.' He grins. And then he adds, with some surprise as if he's just remembered, 'Used to swim for England.

I love you, she says another time. I think I love you. She leans over him.

He pushes himself back on his pillow. I worry you'll get hurt. You need to be more detached. Harder.

I *am* detached, she insists. But hard, no, I don't think I've got it in me. Besides, I don't want to be hard. He swings his legs slowly off the bed. Borrow some of my hardness, he says. I've got enough for us both. Men are bastards, Dana. Something that seems to have passed you by.

TWENTY-FOUR

A fancy-dress party. She borrows a pair of orange-yellow overalls from one of the maintenance guys, a cap to match. When he brings them to the door, the lad lingers, produces a couple of spanners from the pocket of a leather belt at his waist.

'These? You can borrow these too if you want. Put them in your top pocket like. Like this.' He demonstrates. She takes the clothes and the tools, thanks him. But he seems reluctant to leave, stands staring down, drawing in the sand with the steel-capped toe of his boot.

'Is there somewhere I can drop these back? When I've finished with them? Tomorrow morning perhaps.' She smiles at him, but her voice is firm as she steps back into the hall, her hand on the door knob. He'll collect them, he says, around ten the next morning.

Dekker is going as an Arab. He found a red-checked scarf in the *suq* and has taken a lesson from one of the men in the office on how to fold it. On his chin, he's used her eye crayon to draw a goatee beard. She helps him drape a sheet, stands back. He looks quite good, she thinks. Too tall for an Arab, and the beard is too dark. But with his height and his blue eyes it's as if he's stepped out of the *Lawrence of Arabia* film everyone's talking about. All he needs is a camel. And to change his headdress to white with a black plaited band.

'You look good,' she says.

'And you? Where's yours?'

'Here.' She points to the overalls slung over the back of the chair. Then holds them up.

'That? Those?' He grimaces.

'Yes. I'm a handyman.'

He laughs. 'Handy you may be, my dear. But a handyman? Not very feminine. Would you say?'

She laughs too. The moment hangs; he has a look in his eyes she hasn't seen for some time and she thinks for a moment that he is going to move towards her and that she is about to step towards him. But neither of them move. They mirror each other like arrested second hands, jerking towards the next instant. But with the source of energy too weak to jolt them out of the groove they are in, they remain trapped and quivering in the present.

He is about to speak. His mouth opens and he is still looking into her eyes with that strange half-smile. And then he drops his gaze. 'Catch me up?' He turns as if he is about to leave, swings back to face her. Her heart thumps. 'Oh yes, and I may be a bit late home tonight. I've promised to help Rob with the boat. Don't wait up, eh.'

When she turns to pick up her clothes, she feels suddenly tired and she goes through the motions of dressing heavily and rather sluggishly, like a punctured tire. Fights an urge to go to bed instead of going out. I could read, she thinks, have a glass of homebrew. Flat home-made beer. Instead she puts on a white t'shirt, shrugs herself into the overalls, fastens the tiny buckles at the shoulders. It looks like a pair of rompers, she thinks, something that her mother might have worn when she was dating her father, wonders why she so rarely thinks of her parents in that way, why she's never thought of them other than they are.

Since there's so little to put on, she's ready quickly and when she checks her reflection in the mirror she finds herself disagreeing with her husband. The colour suits her and it looks – all right. She is about to turn from the mirror when she tugs off the cap, twists her hair into a knot, rams the cap back on. If she hurries, she can catch him up for a walk across the sand. Why it's suddenly important, she cannot say. The look in his eyes perhaps, a look that has been missing for some time.

Tonight's party is being held to celebrate the recreation hall – Poppy's latest triumph – and the usual crowd is there. They are barely through the door, Dekker ahead of her and making for the drinks table when she is hailed by Erin Richardson wearing a cravat and an eye patch along with his usual open smile.

'It's Dana, isn't it? Just the woman to guess who I am. Failing that, perhaps you would be so good as to indulge in a bit of old-fashioned psychoanalysis.' He steps backwards, strikes a pose, cigarette in one hand, drink in the other. 'I'm a contemporary leader of sorts – famous and infamous – horribly controversial and naturally absolutely brilliant. But if I'm so brilliant, how come I'm not smart enough to avoid contention? Or is the contention in itself a brilliant ploy? Any ideas? Who am I, Dana darling?'

'Not sure I could get it from the character description but, save pirates, not too many figures wear eye patches. Off the top of my head: Moshe Dayan perhaps? Though I shouldn't think he'd affect such a fancy scarf. Or smoke. Or drink anything stronger than holy water.'

'Perhaps he's in fancy dress, the great leader. Doesn't want to be recognized. Perhaps the drink and the smoke are designed to deceive. Do you think? Or is he just confused? Like me?'

'Cheeky, though. To be him. Here.'

'Do you think so?' He raises his eyebrow above the patch. 'More than that man over there dressed as an A-rab?' He nods towards Dekker. 'Appropriation of local identity, that. Tut tut.' He raises the other eyebrow. 'I would have thought that you of all people. Would have thought that in your line of business, you'd find that just as cheeky? Anyway. Be that as it may. Back to Dayan. Think anyone'd make the connection?' Turning on his heel, he exaggerates a scan of the room. 'Anyone, as you said, *here*?'

Erin *is* exaggeration, she thinks. Patronizing too. But having bestowed the phrase 'line of business' upon her, she is willing to forgive him anything. She stands taller.

'Why?' she asks. 'Why are you confused?'

'See? I knew it. Knew you couldn't resist? Said to myself – and myself only, mind you – that Malan girl over-analyses everything. Turns it upside down and inside out. Picks at the stitching, rips the seams, the world to her is just one big tempting scab…'

'You make me sound awful.'

'No, not awful.' For a moment his face loses its boyish openness. Or is it that for once it becomes more serious, just a little? 'Different though, Dana. Different in some way from…a lot of the others. I thought that girl's different the first time I saw you.' He shakes himself like a dog ridding itself of water; his drink spills and his voice changes as he starts talking about the wine club he is setting up. She has not tried wine-making and he advises her to get the Volker kit. 'They sell it at the local shop. Just ask on the QT at the checkout. It's kept on the shelf underneath the cash register along with the hopped malt and the yeast. One of their most reliable sales lines.

'Meanwhile, you don't yet have a drink and you're too polite to say so. So let's wander over and get you one and I'll tell you how to make a *sidiki* still…' He puts one hand on her shoulder, steers her towards the end of the long room. 'The most difficult thing is to get hold of a length of copper tubing…' His words flow over her as she sees Dekker deep in discussion with a Queen of Hearts so tall she can only be Anna and a third figure who might be Anna's husband. And then there's Erin with her drink, but he's barely said, '*Skol*!' before he continues. 'Then you need ten pounds of sugar to four…' Whenever he pauses for breath she tries unsuccessfully to extricate herself until finally he drains his own glass and goes to rejoin the queue. 'Meanwhile old girl, don't forget the wine club.'

She is halfway across the room when a jester sidles up to her, grips her shoulder hard, his thumb digging into her scapula. She winces. He is slender and for a moment she thinks he is the young lad who lent her his overalls. He has the same build and she looks for clues in the colour of the hair that juts out from under the coloured cone on his head, the shape of his mouth and jaw. But the face is plastered with some sort of oily substance, his lips coloured into a bloated and laughing vermillion and his eyes glitter through a series of holes punched in a black mask. He drops his hand from her shoulder, mutters something.

'What?' she asks. 'What's the matter?'

'I said, I asked.' He swallows. 'I asked you what it is that I should do exactly. Or what it is you think I should do. Juggle perhaps? Tumble? Dance? Play chess, maybe? But where's the majesty? No majesty is there? Not his? Or even her? Here to appreciate the fool. In the circumstances.' What words she recognizes out of the slurred phrases delivered in a furious whisper make no sense to her and when he hiccups she realizes he is drunk, very drunk, and she struggles for a clue to his identity in the accent behind the words. 'That's what I am, isn't it? A fool? *The* fool. The king's fool. That's what you see, what she sees, and what you don't see. Don't you see? At all. I don't have to play it, do I? Don't have to pretend. Because it comes naturally. The fool. I don't have to take the mickey out of society, because society does that to itself. Society fucks itself.'

'I don't know what...' She looks around, but there's no one at hand who might help her to encourage him outside. Whoever he may be, he needs help, like being put to bed before he does real damage.

'Help me you too help us. Please. Only you...' His voice wavers. For an instant, he turns his face and palms to the ceiling before he dashes the knuckles of one hand into the palm of the other, the light glistening off the wetness on the greasy paint of his cheeks. And then, shrugging off her hand as she goes to stop him, he moves away as suddenly as he appeared, heading rapidly towards the door with, to her surprise, no sign of swaying or lurching, no unsteadiness of movement, rather the opposite. Who is he? The way he walks – that leonine tread – stirs something in her memory. Was he waiting for her? Did he intend to meet her here? And if so, what did it all mean? Because whether he's drunk or drugged or terribly upset it's obvious he needs help of some kind. Dekker will know what to do.

She makes her way through the crowd, oblivious of those who would stop her now, reaches Dekker just as Anna waves to her and moves off down the hall. She still wears the crown, tilted slightly towards one eyebrow, but she has discarded the red crepe cloak and is dressed now in a slithery sheath dress of silver-gold. The cast-off mantle leaks scarlet into a spill of punch.

'What?' says Dekker when she's finished telling him. He grins. 'Stop a man drinking? An infringement of civil rights. Whoever he is, I'm quite sure he's able to take care of himself,' he continues. 'And if he's not, he's hardly your responsibility. Eh? Don't nanny people, Dana.'

She wants to say that it's not like that, that he hasn't understood what she has been trying to say, that it's not simply a matter of inebriation but something else, something she can't quite put her finger on. But he goes to run his hands through his hair, finds to his annoyance he is still wearing the headdress. Tilts the empty glass in his hand.

'Going to top up,' he says. He glances at her half glass. 'And you?'

She shakes her head, wonders whether she read all the signs wrong just an hour earlier. But obviously now is not the time to talk. She pretends she sees someone she needs to speak to the other side of the room, smiles lightly as she turns away.

The party has thinned out and Dekker has already left to help Rob by the time she decides she's ready for home. As she steps outside the hall, she finds to her surprise that it's lighter outside. The moon is nearly full and the night is full of shadows.

'Uh, you're leavin'. Already. And there I was, hopin' to catch you.' Tay in her path. He stops, rests his foot on a slab of limestone and stands looking down at her.

'You're not dressed,' she remarks. 'Not fancy-dressed that is.'

'No.' There's a smile in his eyes, not on his lips. 'Don't go in for that sort of thing.'

Something rises in her. She bites it back. The memory of their disagreement is still strong and she doesn't want to step back into it. She tries for lightness, but there's an edge to her words. 'Then, why come at all. What are you doing here? You don't usually come to parties.'

'As I said.' He leans his elbow on his raised knee, rubs his chin. 'I was hopin' to catch you.'

It unsettles her, to see him unexpectedly in the night like this, his head outlined against the starry sky. You care, she wants to say. I think you actually do care. But in some part of her she knows that it is not quite true that he cares. Or if he does, that there is some sort of parallel truth which changes the nature of the caring. She knows he has sensed what she is thinking.

His eyes are steady. Quite gentle. But she starts at his words. 'I blame your parents for you.'

'Blame my parents? What on earth for?'

'For you being the way you are.'

'If you were a drinker, I'd say you'd been drinking.'

He shakes his head. 'Something about you altogether too trusting, too needy.'

'Me? Needy!' It's so light she suspects he can see her face flame. 'Being an only child, I've actually spent great tracts of time by myself, for your information. As for trusting, you don't head up a team of...'

'It's not that sort of trust I'm talkin' of. You kid yourself too much. Seems to me you're living in a bit of a bubble. Too controlled. And I worry what'll happen to you when it bursts. As bubbles tend to. I fear for you Dana.'

'You! Worry about me.' She snorts. 'Don't bother. I don't know what you're on about suddenly. But if it's anything to do with what I said the other day...'

He bends towards her. 'What I'm on about is that you need a reality check. Those parents of yours don't seem to have left you with enough self-value. You've been taught to respect everyone's opinion but your own. You need to have a bit of faith in yourself. If you go to bed with a man, go to bed with him to show *how little* respect you have for him, not *how much*.'

'Finished with the lecture?' Her voice is cold. She goes to walk on, spins back. 'Why are you saying this? Suddenly. Right here. Why now?'

'Because you need to hear it. Because you need to wake up. Before you do yourself some harm. You're so intent on playing it safe. Doin' the right thing by everybody. You're trapped Dana. But it's not this joint that's trapped you. It's you not thinkin' for yourself. Yes, I blame your parents in the first place. Knocked a bit too much out of you. But at some point, you're going to need to stand up for yourself.'

'Oh for heaven's sake,' she snaps and she is about to say more when he stops her. He nods at her outfit.

'Becomes you.' But his tone is curt, no warmth in it. She shrugs, moves away. He swings his foot down, falls in step.

She tries to match his detachment, tries for coolness. 'I thought.' She gestures towards the din behind them.

'Like I said. Only reason for comin' out was to meet you.' He walks her to the end of her short pathway, smiles briefly and turns into the night. She forces herself not to look back as she lets herself into the house.

Still trying to work out what he means about neediness and trust, she falls asleep and is only dimly aware of Dekker finally arriving home, showering and getting into bed beside her. Her dreams are full of court jesters and their Queens with golden crowns askew. And handymen playing at being something they aren't.

They both wake early, so early in fact that Dana wonders whether Dekker has been to sleep at all. He lies quite still and straight so his feet stick out of the sheets at the end of the bed, his eyes staring at the ceiling.

'So,' he says.

'So what?'

'Well, this trip we've discussed. We have to book today and we need to know how many to book for. In other words, have you decided whether to come or not?'

'We?'

'To make up the four of us.'

'A foursome? To Greece. Or back home?'

'Sometimes, Dana, you can be very slow.' He moves his feet irritably. 'We discussed it. Going to the Greek islands. Remember. Just the other day.'

'We discussed four?'

'Anna and John want to come with us.'

'Anna?' She lifts her head from the pillow. 'I don't believe this.'

'What isn't there to believe, eh? I thought she was a friend of yours?'

'But you – you just go ahead and arrange something like this. And then. And then you present it to me as a *fait accompli*?'

'You didn't sound very keen to me. In fact, I clearly remember you saying…'

'No, I wasn't keen. And I was surprised because the only place we'd discussed until the other day was back to the Cape for a holiday. To see the folks. And then suddenly it was a pile of fancy pictures of bright boats and hot rocks. And now someone else sharing the trip.'

'Not just someone, another couple.'

She swings her feet out of the bed. 'And last night. Last night before we went out, I almost thought. For a moment there I thought we could be back as we once were.' She closes her eyes, draws a deep breath. 'It doesn't matter.'

For the first time, he turns his head. Gazes at her steadily. 'What's good for the goose, Dana.'

She stares at him. 'But it was you. It was you who distanced yourself. It was you first. You pushed me away. It was fine at first, when I first got here.' The way he had taken her in his arms at the airport. *Too long*, he'd said. *Much, much too long.*

'You took so long to get here.' He goes back to studying the ceiling.

'The jester, the clown at the thing last night. He was Anna's husband, wasn't he? I didn't recognize him at the time. Only later. The way he walked. But you knew, didn't you? Is that why you did nothing?' Bright sparks chasing across her brain.

He raises himself onto his elbow. 'I've told you before. Don't interfere in things you know nothing about.'

'And you. You're not interfering, I suppose, in someone else's marriage.' Her body is shaking. He looks so smug. She wants to kill him.

I'm thinking of leaving Dekker. It bursts out of her the next time she sees Tay.

He jerks his head. Puts the teapot down in the middle of pouring. Thought the other day you were on about balance? That sounds abrupt and very unbalanced to me. I thought you two were getting on a lot better these days?

We are and we aren't. This is not what either of us want for the rest of our lives. She looks straight into his eyes. Let's face it, I wouldn't be here, chatting with you if my marriage was working. And besides he's having an affair. It started, I've only just realized, before I even arrived.

He shrugs. Have you tried asking him what he wants?

She drops to the carpet, tucks her legs under her. He won't talk. He doesn't talk.

He nods. Men tend not to. If they can help it. Talk that is.

And when he does, he says things like one should die when one marries and that your responsibilities own you.

He chuckles. It's a male thing. What worries me about you is that you over-react. Try to go with the flow a little more.

When she thinks flow, she thinks of the dirty stream that runs through the centre of al-Dhuraf. She thinks of the shopping trip with Anna, Anna's silences, Anna pressed up against her in the crush, Anna buying yet more bangles, Anna frenetic. And how she stood waiting for Anna, watching the stream, marveling that not only were there fish swimming among the flotsam, but also that they were surviving. She thinks particularly of the lone fingerling swimming in the opposite direction to the rest, wonders whether it ever made it to its destination. Or whether it lived to regret the urge that made it turn the other way, to fight its way upstream, or whether eventually it too turned to take the easy way out, to follow the tide.

And he thinks – or rather he says that a person is a wife first and a person second. I wish, she says savagely, that more men thought and talked the way you do.

'Ware these feet of clay, he murmurs. How's the paintin' coming along then?

I'm not sure it is, she says shortly. Even to Tay she can't admit the one work of art she's ever done that is any good at all is of her husband's lover.

That's a pity. Why not?

She shrugs.

You don't look like a quitter to me.

Who said anything about quitting? It's not a question of quitting, she snaps.

I thought that was what you were gettin' at.

It's just this whole set-up here. Money. Bloody money. All these clever women doing what? Tennis, bridge, collecting sea shells, desert roses. Painting, trying to paint or pretending to paint or draw or write. She snorts. There is a patriarchy here, you know…

Of course there is. What took you so long to figure that?

Oh Tay. She shakes her head. I so want my old job back. The painting – yes, I know I was fired up – an endeavour to make something of my time here, to make it work for me. But…I don't think I have the talent. Maybe I need lessons or something.

He gets up. Phff. Talent. Lessons. He bites at the words so they rear up in front of her like a striking snake. I don't really think you believe that. Like I keep saying, I blame your parents for you. I don't think you think things through. Properly.

Sometimes I hate you. She rises from the floor, dusts off the back of her long skirt, slips her feet into her sandals. I really hate you.

That's a relief. B'n wonderin' what I was going to do should you suffer another bout of sudden affection.

She bangs the metal door behind her, glares at the row of houses shimmering in the noon day heat, all of them floating somewhere between heaven and hell.

His words sting. And keep stinging along the path to home. So when she gets in the door she goes straight for the canvas and sketchpads, brings them down with a crash and carries them into the little garden. She works first on the pads, ripping out the pages and tearing them again and again. Then she jumps on the canvas, rushes inside for scissors and cut into the stiff board until her hand is bruised and bits of Anna lie here and there all over the sand. Her helpless mouth, drawn tight around a cigarette, or open in a rare deprecating laugh, mocking, a smile of scorn, straight taut lips. Eyes, the inward-focused eyes, the sheet of hair she hides behind, whether twisted into a roll or hanging loose, ready always to come to her defence. But it gives her away too. All parts of Anna expose and exposed. All parts of Anna inextricable from her actions. Like the bangles. That so suit her, that raft of golden circles. The unceasing jingle. The ease with which they ride each other up and down her thin tanned arm. The furious noise that must exist inside her head.

Perhaps the only thing she has ever drawn that had some merit. She pictures Peter Novotny pulling at his neat beard as he gazes at it. Using his contempt as fuel, she doesn't notice the time.

TWENTY-FIVE

There is nothing remarkable in the way she meets Tay's regular bridge partner and it's only later she wonders whether it was quite the coincidence it seemed at the time. She's mounted the wooden steps to the mezzanine level of the local store, and is moving gingerly on the sloping floor between the aisles when she trips over a loose board. Her basket of groceries tips and the cans start rolling like a table of pinballs.

'Oops.' A high-heeled shoe shoots out, an ankle curves around a tin of tomatoes about to tip over the edge. 'Caught that one!' The woman bends to help her and when they rise up laughing to face each other, says, 'Anyway, saved those people down there from a bang on the head.' She taps her forehead. 'Correct me perhaps. But I think you are Dana. The wife of Dekker Malan. Yes?'

She is not sure how she knows in this instant that this is Katya, with hair not quite brown, not quite blond, cut short and shaped to enhance the tilt of her nose.

The woman extends her hand. 'Kat Abercrombie is my name. We share a friendship with Taylor, I think. Am I right?'

'Katya? Taylor's bridge partner?'

'Yes, Katya. Kat, too. Which is my, how do you say it, pet name?'

No make-up. No need for make-up. She tries not to think of Tay sitting across from her each week, maybe more than once a week. Her fingernail traces the embossing on one of the cans. Why go to the trouble of embossing a can? For aesthetics? Strength? But the other woman is smiling broadly.

'Can you come across to my house for a cup of coffee? Just half an hour. For a quick chat? I live on the other side of the camp from you, a bit too far to walk in a short time but my car is outside.'

Dana glances at her watch. *Don't go*, clicks the second hand, *don't go*. But there's a reason she has bumped into this woman just now.

'All right. Thank you. But I have a driver and I'm just about finished here. I can follow.'

Aside from being set away from the others to the rear of the camp, Katya's house is no different from any of the others on the outside. But as she steps into the hallway at the entry to the lounge, she stops still.

'I've never,' she says slowly, 'seen anything so…wow! Or maybe only once before – my parents-in-law's house in Constantia – '

Katya drops her bag on the kitchen island, flicks the switch on the kettle. 'All the work of Christopher, I'm afraid. All of it. Sometimes I think it's too much. All this stuff crammed in here. But he's always collected. So we continue to collect. He's the creative one. Wasted here as an engineer. I keep telling him he should be in design. Maybe, one day, if we return to London.' She lifts her shoulders lightly. 'If you want, take your time. Look around while I make this.'

'London?' Dana says into the space. She isn't English. Russian perhaps? Polish? She rotates slowly on her heels, her gaze soaking up the vitality, the juxtaposition of artifacts, the fineness of the silk hangings on the walls along with the portraits of men and women who stare out of heavy black frames, the Persian carpets on the floor, the brass, copper and silver pots, vases and urns. A dizzying blend of ornament that somehow works. She sits on the couch of cream patterned silk. No children here. No dogs or cats or chocolate fingers.

'One day, yes. Always one day we'll return. That's how we live here. From day to day.' She hands Dana a cup, fine china, liquid deep and dark and still swirling, the bitter aroma lifting on the steam. 'Cream? Sugar?'

Usually she has her coffee black and unsweetened, but it's been so long since she had real cream that she heaps it on, spoons a sprinkle of coloured crystals on top. This, too, is art, a still life, this careless arrangement of the soft pastels cast across the thick cream. As Katya seats herself on the couch opposite, her cup balancing lightly on her knee, the spell is broken; she has to restrain herself from looking at her watch, knows that the time which was always going to be either too short or too long is racing away.

'Taylor,' says Katya. 'Well, what I would like to know is what you think of him?'

Dana sidesteps. 'But why haven't I seen you around? Why has it taken so long to meet?'

Katya smiles crisply. 'A lot of the time we are out of town, here and there. All over the world really. But here, Christopher is a consultant. You see? Consultant to the consultants. We don't mix so much while we are here. Some bridge, perhaps. That's all.' She laughs. 'But, my question?'

'What I think of Taylor?' Dana shakes herself out of her daze.

'I'm wondering. How much do you know of this man?'

'Well.' Dana crosses and re-crosses her feet and then shifts them again. 'Well, he's a friend. I know him well enough.'

'Nice man. He speaks well of you. And often. So I feel I've met you already.' A quick smile before she looks down to stir her coffee. 'I know him quite well. Very well, perhaps. I think I can almost say that. Over the course of three or maybe four years.' In the curtained window of time available, the discussion, Dana realizes suddenly, is going to be all about Tay. 'He's told you about us?'

'Yes, of course he has. That you play a lot of bridge together. His regular partner. I'm afraid I don't stack up too well alongside you.' Her smile locks.

'Well, as I said, we've been partnering each other for quite some time now. So it's only natural we know each other's game.' She shrugs. 'But there's a little bit more. Did he tell you the rest? That he wants...' She breaks off, grimaces. 'So silly really. That he wishes to live with me when we leave here?' She laughs. 'It's a bit of fiction in his mind, I think.'

'Live with you?' Dana struggles to keep her face neutral, her voice sounds as if it's coming from a long way away, bubbled through a drill pipe to the surface of the earth. 'Live with you? But I thought he was married. I'm sorry. I'm…a bit confused.'

Katya laughs again, more of a chuckle. She could have been talking about getting a pet dog. It's hard to take her seriously. On the other hand, there is no doubt she is serious.

'Yes, of course. We both are a bit confused. But you see, that doesn't stop this dream of his. He wants me to live with him in London.'

'In London.' She is talking – and hearing – through this ridiculous conduit connected somewhere a long way away.

'Yes, in London. He wants to set me up in a small flat somewhere. Me! Can you imagine it?' The laughter again. 'Completely impossible, of course. But I think most dreams are, aren't they? Which is why they work best as dreams.' She raises her shoulders delicately, gives Dana a sideways smile as she takes a sip. 'No reflection on Taylor. But naturally it wouldn't work. He is married anyway of course. As you say. Men!'

'And.' Dana clears her throat. 'Your husband. Does he know?'

'We have had long discussions…' An alarm sounds from somewhere in the house. Katya glances at the clock and groans. 'Oops, the time already gone. Never enough time.' She tips the rest of the cup down her throat and sets the cup down. Dana rises at the signal. She knows she should say something. Something like, Why are you telling me all this? What business is this of mine? Her own coffee sits untouched on the coffee table. The pretty crystals have sunk or dissolved and the cream is now the colour of dirty brown. Droplets of yellow oil cluster on the surface.

She keeps the smile on her face all the way to the car, winds down the window to wave airily at the figure standing in front of the house.

'Home please, Mr. Kim.' Her faces aches. Despite the blinding heat of the day, her hands are cold.

TWENTY-SIX

The date stamp fascinates her. First it is the regularity with which she has to change the date almost as if the little lever itself is responsible for the speed with which the days click over. Then there's the surprisingly tactile pleasure she gets from the simple action of pressing it evenly onto the ink pad, and the satisfaction of seeing the clean imprint placed so exactly between the lines on the ruled sheets pasted into the front of the books. It's only a date stamp, a bloody date stamp, she tells herself, but she knows she is lying and that it is more than that, that it means more to her than that. It means that time is passing. And at the moment she doesn't know whether that is good or bad.

It's past closing time. But there's something that's keeping her here. She stares at the stamp. Thinks about leaving a note for Poppy. She has to see Poppy. When suddenly she's there pulling up a chair to the other side of the small table.

'Lovely surprise. Where's Ruf?'

'School. Playschool. Crèche. I'm not quite sure what it is. Not sure how Edwin Priddle copes with the mix of ages. He's got the whole gamut there now from two-year-olds through to senior school. And he's trying to manage with inadequate books and teaching tools for such a range of ages and disparate bunch of kids. I'm trying to get him some help. Among all these bored women, Dana, wouldn't you think someone would put up her hand?'

'Maybe. No, not maybe. Yes, you're right. I don't know why they don't. Except your mind gets kind of snap-frozen after being here for a while. Misses the obvious.'

Poppy shrugs. 'Meanwhile, Dana. Advice please. Not something I often ask for. But I need to know what you think about this.' She sorts through her handbag and draws out a piece of folded notepaper which she hands to Dana. And then she glances down, rubs at an invisible mark on her skirt. 'What do you think,' she says again.

Dana starts to read.

If a lovely girl comes to see me out of the blue in the middle of the night – that is one thing.

She looks up from the letter. 'But this is private, Poppy,' she says. 'Are you sure you want to share stuff like this?'

'Yes, yes, I am. I want to know what you think of it.'

'You're okay though?'

'Yes, yes.' Poppy moves impatiently.

Dana spreads out the thin sheet. The signature at the bottom. 'David? Poppy, what is this?'

Poppy shrugs. 'Carry on.'

You're one in a million, believe me. BUT you are also so much, so very much more than that — and that fact was what worried me even when we were together you see. Plus Ronnie — let's be honest.

'Ronnie?'

'Ronnie — or it's Veronica really — she's his fiancée, you see; they marry sometime in the next little while and then he plans to bring her out here. He — they — are going to be living in the house in front of mine. In other words, my lounge looks out onto the patio he's in process of having bricked.'

Dana picks up the letter again. Poppy's gaze on her.

As a matter of interest if a simple sexy chick did come a-knocking it would be wham-bam, thank you ma'am and cheerio. But you are a very special sort of person and you should really love and be loved. Life is unfair to Women. But they are the stronger sex inside. That's me being pompous again. I would like to talk to you for hours and make lots of love to you too — but I can't have everything darn it. I am very lucky to have someone of my very own at last. But you want a friend, Poppy? I do. See you when I get back to camp. David

Fountain pen, good paper. Firmly she refolds it, runs her finger and thumb hard together along the fold line.

'That's David Devenish, isn't it? Him and you. Christ.' She reaches for recollection. The first time she met him. Her first or second day on camp. What had Poppy said? Something about old tricks? About his being up to his old tricks. And Tay? What had he said? Poppy's got some influence I believe.

'Yes. As you say, Christ.'

'For long?'

'Almost as long as I've been here. As long as we've both – he and I – have been here. Years now, I guess.'

'Does…Laurie know?'

'Oh yes, Laurie knows. Laurie knows everything. In fact, you could say Laurie encouraged it in the first place. He knew from the beginning that it would be the only way to keep me – or more pertinently, let's face it – to keep his son here in these surroundings and that with the best will in the world I would go completely loopy cooped up behind this wall without some sort of outlet. And, believe me, there was not much outlet of any shape or kind when we first got here. Besides he…' She shakes her head. 'Well, let's just say that for one reason or another the arrangement suited him fine. It still does, to tell the truth.'

'And the…baby?'

'David's.'

'Heck, Poppy.'

'It could have been, yes.'

'Meaning?'

'Well, if the babe had gone to term, it would have course…been difficult. Very difficult indeed. Although at the time it was what I wanted, of course, to have the baby. More than anything, more than anything else in the entire world. But it wasn't to be.' She bites down on her bottom lip, her eyes fixed on a small fly hovering towards the ceiling.

Dana presses her hands together. 'But how can I help? *Can* I help?'

'Only that I need someone to fess up to, someone I can tell all this to. We all know everyone here, but they come and go, as you know, like the proverbial desert sands and we have few real friends.'

She folds the note again, twice, so it's a small square of white paper that she tucks quickly into her bag. Dana wonders at the absurdity of the image that pops into her mind of the childhood game of forecast and fortune hidden in the paper pop-up you manipulated with thumb and forefinger.

But Poppy is saying, 'I understand I have to accept this – David and Ronnie – and that it was always going to happen. It was just a question of when, which always seemed very distant and unreal. But it's real now. It's happened.' She smoothes her creaseless skirt. 'Playing with fire and all that. I've seen her, his fiancée, you know. Seen her the other side of the room when she visited once. About a year ago. And then apart from her photo beside his bed which he turns to the wall whenever I'm with him, she sort of disappeared. Until now.' Her gaze somewhere beyond the ceiling. 'And the point is, until now I've been able to handle it. Convinced myself that I was one of the new women to whom sex means as little as it seems to with men. That I could just walk away when it was over. After all, I'm married too.

'But now – suddenly I'm not so sure I can. Not sure that I can face her living slap bang in front of me, seeing her all the time.' Her hands twist. 'I'm just not sure how to handle things. I absolutely have to find something intelligent to occupy my time, Dana. The library's fine. But it's not enough. What do I do? Do I stay? Do I leave? For a long holiday? For good? Laurie'll never leave. I know that now. So it'll mean raising Ruf on my own, without a Dad. Or with a part-time father. And then, all this – all these years I've been here – will have been for nothing. It breaks my heart that after all this time, we're no further forward than we were years ago. The same problems re-presenting themselves. Except messier and messier.'

Think, Dana tells herself. What I need is Tay. What *we* need is Tay. He must have known about David all along. Perhaps I was the only one who didn't? How little, how much can I say? How can I help this person whose eyes are still on the ceiling, whose lips are folded so tight they've disappeared, who is unaware of her hands ironing her skirt?

'Does it help,' she starts. And then, 'I wonder whether it helps in the slightest to know that we're all in this together. Sometimes – sometimes when my mind is too messed up to sleep – I sit at the dining room table. Just sit. And sooner or later someone will cross the sand – usually the figure of a woman, sometimes a man – sometimes two or three in the hour I might sit there. They're suddenly there and then gone, disappearing so quickly between the houses that sometimes I wonder whether I've imagined them. Until in the morning – sometimes the dents are still there in the sand. A lot of us being too brave. Thinking that the world has really changed. Believing that now – somebody, society, something – has made it okay to jump from one bed to another. Telling ourselves and each other that we can just do this and move on when it suits us. But somewhere along the line, we've forgotten that we're not machines. And, you know, I'm not so sure that it's always so easy for men either? Maybe some men. Maybe some women. But I think there are others of both sexes that allow themselves to feel hurt or regret or indecision. We just get ourselves in a rotten tangle in the meantime.' She spreads her hands.

'Perhaps it's something that only time can fix. I don't really know what to say…'

There's only the clock echoing like a gong as Poppy's gaze comes down off the ceiling. She looks at her restless hands as if she's never seen them before, folds them as firmly as she had the letter, drops them in her lap.

'It helps. A bit. Of course it does. But, oh, Dana, two lonely people – and now I'm talking Laurie and me – who think they're the bees knees at coping with the loneliness of being on a camp miles away from family. And most of the time we can. Most of the time it's all right. It's only just sometimes it gets too hard. And then. And then you let someone else inside your head with you. Which can be a bad mistake. As it turns out.'

Yes, a mistake, Dana says to herself. And yet? Aloud she says, 'We're all out of place here, Poppy. Out of our comfort zones. It's all so unreal and forced and controlled. We're out of place – and something in me says that I too am running out of time.' She shrugs and later she thinks it's more the uncertainty in this impatient movement of her shoulders than her actual words that shifts Poppy's attention.

'Out of time? Meaning? Exactly?'

Dana sighs. 'Nothing exact, nothing concrete, nothing cast in stone and I'm not even sure when. Or even why I feel it. But I think the time is coming when I'm going to have to leave here myself. It's getting on for nine months. I'm getting progressively used to doing nothing. But it's not me. It doesn't suit me. Dekker has decided he will stay on.'

Last night, at the table after dinner Dekker talking again about the Greek trip. Which he'd booked. The three of them. Three, she had said. Which three? 'Well, you certainly didn't seem too interested. So I went ahead and booked for myself and the others.' She'd said in that case, she thought it was time for her to leave, to return to Johannesburg. He nodded as if he had known this all along. But he will stay on, he said, for a while. 'But if you wish to go home, as you still call it, then why not, eh?' She was unprepared for his ready agreement. Expected he would try to change her mind. But now, finding somewhere to live, a new job. Alone? How long, she had asked then, how long before you join me? But he moved his dinner plate aside, looked down at his clasped hands. 'I haven't yet finished here, Dana. Too many loose ends. I can't leave right now.' She knows all about loose ends. Has quite a few herself. But for how long? For how much longer will you be here? Do you think? Wanting an answer, keeping her words, her voice, her tone, deliberately flat and unchallenging. 'A few months, six maybe, a year at the outside. No longer. By then, financially, we will be well set up.' Is it the money, she asked. Only the money? He stood up from the table. 'What else would it be?'

She had risen then, too. Collected up the plates roughly. It could perhaps be the Queen of Hearts. It could be that you don't want to leave with me. It could be that you're still undecided whether to relocate to Australia or to return to South Africa or whether to go somewhere quite different. It could perhaps be that you want to set yourself up with a mistress in London. Or, yes indeed, it could be the job. Or the job as well. If you don't tell me, how do I know? But if I say any of this – and I didn't say it aloud, did I? – you will sigh and shake your head and turn away just as you are doing now and I will walk out of the house and run around and around inside the wall, my body vibrating along with the beating of my heart, my shoes thumping on the damp night sand. A trotter on an outside track. Losing ground with every stride. Going nowhere. Going backwards in the river of horses. But doing it with the most incredible energy and focus.

Poppy's gaze is steady now and Dana meets it as she says, 'I've learned – heaps – from here. But you know, Poppy, it's been nothing like I thought it would be. A chance to see Arabia, to see something of the country, to mix with the Arabs and learn a bit about their culture first hand. Remember our first meeting? Christ, it seems like years ago. Nothing like that at all. Glimpses, that's all.

'I saw – when I first arrived here – I saw a woman staring out from behind a grill of a sort of basement flat in al-Khasi village. Her eyes level with the street. Music – clear separate notes – floating past her head out through the window. The music somehow part of her – and for that fraction of an instant part of me too – although it wasn't something she was playing. Or even appeared to be listening to. But her eyes were greedy; there was something in them that's stayed with me. It wasn't loneliness. Nor anger. Not even frustration. A wanting or desire of some sort. Or maybe she was just absorbing her street view so she could play it back to herself later. Or it could be she was dreaming, far away from the heaps of rat-infested rubbish and the barred window.

'Funny. I had forgotten her until now. What I saw was more than just a shadowy image of a heavily-garbed woman looking out into the street. She must have a story. And that was part of what I wanted to do here. Paint the story of my time here. Draw it even. Away from the folks with no pressure to perform, just let the work flow, either to prove my father wrong or to prove to myself I could do it. Or both. A chance to free up my creative side. But it didn't work out like that. Because I wanted to do it for the wrong reasons perhaps?' She shakes her head. 'Besides what do we see of the Arabs anyway? Just shapes in the market place carrying their baskets. Or smarter in the city, women with their eyes and lips made up, finger nails polished, their *abayas* made of expensive stuff that swings with them as they move instead of dragging them down.' She draws in her breath, lets it out slowly. Picks up a book from the centre of the table, stares unseeing at the cover.

'I don't know what else I thought it would be like here other than having a warm and fuzzy time with Dekker. But the Dekker I know is…distant. He's gone to a place where he doesn't want to be disturbed. Or not by me anyway.'

'It's all gone a bit pear-shaped, wouldn't you say,' says Poppy.

'And that's only half of it. And then there's Taylor.'

TWENTY-SEVEN

Uncertain still as to whether she will leave or not, she starts to plan her leaving party regardless. She will have a dinner, she thinks. Over the time she has been here, there have been scores of gatherings, darts and slide evenings, but few dinner parties. She will borrow another table so they can seat ten people. Cover the tables with a length of white and gold brocade she has seen at the market. Stand bunches of her oleanders with their white flowers and fresh green leaves in glasses down the centre. Dekker is a competent cook and he has perfected a specialty. Roast duck that he bones with infinite patience, fills with stuffing and stuffs again with oranges through the middle. And then it's trussed with leg bones restored, so it looks once again like a duck. This is something he does exceptionally well. Makes something that's had its skeleton removed look like it hasn't changed a bit. As they have so often said, he could have moved seamlessly into the museum world of painstaking restoration. Three or four of these ducks will form the main course, the centre-point of the dinner where the carving of the birds is in itself a party trick. She will work the rest of the menu around that. In the snug of her garden, she works on a list.

It is nearly two weeks after her visit to Katya's house that she pays her last visit to the row of transportables. Every day she has been expecting to run into Taylor and when each day she doesn't, she tells herself that he must have seen Katya and that it's his sense of guilt keeping him away. At first her pride and anger is enough to stop her from visiting and then one night it is no longer enough.

The light is on over his front door; she knows he is home. She knocks softly. Taps on the door. Telling herself in the moment of stillness she is expecting nothing other than his usual welcome, the lidded eyes with the smile tucked into the corners, the door flung wide.

Once she had started to think more clearly, she realized that she did not know how much truth, if any, there was in what she had been told. How much of it was mischief. Or jealousy. Or both. Katya's story was in equal measure both plausible and improbable and in retrospect Dana mistrusts the all too convenient juxtaposition of events, the coincidence of meeting her and being invited back to her home. How easily she had allowed herself to be led. How readily she had suffocated any misgivings at the time. How easily she has been to lay blame, and yet here she is, just as ready to bury the anger, to make excuses for him.

She raps on the door again. More loudly. Waits, calls softly. She is tempted to try the handle. But if it is locked? That's one humiliation she couldn't bear to face. But she taps then on the window, the window above his bed. Pictures him lying there in the dark, naked, hands folded behind his head on the single pillow listening to her growing frustration, feeling her anger seep through the thin metal of the van. As he stares at Jane Avril's black-stockinged leg and thinks again of swapping it for the Lady Godiva on her silver pony. Imagining this. Imagining him. Invective rising now too quickly through her body meeting a blackness coming downwards to settle over her.

She fights to breathe normally, wants to shriek and destroy, to run through the camp with a knife. If indeed she has been too contained, the lock has surely rusted out.

Just in time, she turns aside and it is not reason that causes her to do so. It is some other thing, something ephemeral like a leaf caught on the breeze, something so flimsy that even as she reaches to grasp it, hang on to it, it dissolves. Borrow some of my hardness, he'd said. Beware these feet of clay, he'd said. Men are bastards. His words hang in front of her. Black writing, block letters on white paper suspended in the air in front of her eyes. She didn't believe him then. Still doesn't. Not sure she believes the woman either. Too smooth, too ready with her story. Can't see them together. She rubs her hands uneasily. She has something special with Tay. It's not the sex. Not just the sex. The so unimportant sex. And yet. Isn't that, too, part of the frisson between them? All the times they'd had. The talks and the listening. The narrow bed, the tiny window.

She turns away. Faces the houses that look back at her, their lights veiled. How much can they see looking out into the dark? More than a shadow on a night as light as tonight, the moon smugly full and lighting up the pathways. She forces herself to walk away from the run of cabins, two rows deep. Walks to the wall. Finds the prickly finish of the rough-cast concrete as hostile as Sodom.

I hate you, she says to the big wall. The concrete blocks echo back at her. Borrow some of my hardness. The trouble with you. Ten riyals. Ten riyals is the fine for a man, but for a woman... A sudden surge of blood blocks her throat like vomit and the fight leaves her as quickly as it arrived.

The lights of the houses glow unsteadily, winking a little like stars. It is early still with the camp not yet turned in for the night. There she goes, they will be saying behind the trembling lace of the curtains, the mad woman of al-Khasi walking the walk. Yet again.

She strides quickly, head down. It's only when she finds herself in the measureless space outside the camp walls looking back at the rows of squat houses that she realizes this is the first time she has been out through the gates by herself. Gates which, when she comes to think of it, she has never seen closed. Up close they are either gigantic or she's shrunk. Like Alice. One moment she was in, now she's out. All of a sudden she's shivering violently and it's due to more than the hint of chill in this month of September. You rant and rail against the loathsome restriction of prison, said Poppy, but if you are in for any length of time, you're lost once you're set free. But the further she walks, the taller she feels and when she glances back over her shoulder at the compound, she is surprised to find that it is this that now looks scaled down. As if it's been made from Ruf's Lego as it hunkers down behind its wall.

It's only when she becomes aware that her breath has returned to even, that her pace has slowed to an amble that she stops, sinks to the ground. Sand cold as a slab of granite and almost as unyielding. Quite unlike the shifting sands of the compound. Slightly damp. Maybe she'll get piles. Despite herself, she grins. Where did that come from? Her mother? From long ago, wet bathers, concrete pool surrounds. A snap of guilt, so long since she thought of her mother. Even longer since she wrote to her. And now, when she goes back, what will they think of her? Instead of returning with her husband, happily pregnant, with some well-executed paintings in her cases and a host of Middle Eastern travels to talk about, she is about to return alone, unemployed and barren. Expectations fulfilled, father. Except I bet even you couldn't have predicted it would end like this. Crumpled chopped-up bits of Anna's face on a canvas being nibbled away by rats on heaven knows what tip.

End? Like this? Feels as if she is about to explode. She digs into the sand with her fingernails. Forces herself to examine options. Options. There is always an option. Your choice, he had said. She had chosen to do what she had done. Coming here in the first place, that too she had chosen. Hadn't she examined and analysed, looked at the situation from every angle, decided finally that she missed Dekker too much to delay further? But the truth of the matter was that she had delayed too long already.

Her fingers dig so the crystals cut into her fingers. She breathes. Closer to Dekker's mother than her own. But then she doesn't know her own mother; she'd never been someone you could get close to. Perhaps that was because there was always her father in the way. When she thinks about it, her mother has lived in the shadow of her father much as a house might crouch down in the foothills of a mountain. Always her father's rules that she abided by, her father who gave or withheld praise or pocket money or punishment. Not the bad kind, this last; he didn't have to. One look was enough to stop the bities mid-dance. I blame your parents. Is that what Tay means? But isn't responsibility a two-way thing? And how can he blame them when he doesn't know any of this?

She digs deeper. Good sand for sandcastles. But you need children for those. And the prospect of that is about as close as the speck on the horizon that's all that's left of the camp.

Good sand to write on. It was on sand like this that Qays wrote his verses. All the time going mad. Had the poetry helped, she wonders. Staved off the moment he crossed that thin almost imperceptible line between being sane and insane. A division that lay somewhere on a slippery scale between rational and irrational. Between logic and illogic. Is it fair that an arbiter on one side of that scale should judge for both? That a judge is assumed sane when he makes an evaluation between sane and insane? Who judges the judge? How far has the judge travelled along that narrow winding road between one state and another? Is there more empathy for the insane from a judge who has travelled along that path? Who dares draw that fragile line in the sand? And who dares step over it?

Her fingers strike something hard, rough, a rock perhaps. She looks down, surprised to find she's dug quite a hole, uses her other hand now to work around the edge of what she thinks may be a desert rose. It sucks hard into its bed of sand, reluctant to let go and it's some time before she is able to tug it out. She traces the outline of the overlapping pieces of crystal. 'Crystallised gypsum and sand, these desert roses. Find them in parts once flooded by the sea. Worth something if you can get a good one.' She's forgotten the name of the woman who collects shells and has a whole bookshelf of such roses. She turns it upside-down, taps it lightly with her hand, blows softly to release sand still too damp to shift. But she can see enough of it shining silver as any star to know that this is a particularly fine example.

She holds it in her lap cupped in both hands. Still now. Still enough to look up, the moon so close she can reach up and stroke it, the sky midnight blue, translucent, the light so strong it turns the sand the colour of ice. Where has it been, the moon, these last months? Blanked out by the sun? The night air is motionless and cool. But she is not cold, too much anger in her still for that. Apart from the camp, the only breaks in the smooth line of the horizon are the flares of the rigs. She can see two, a third further away. Somewhere there's a road, she knows, but if it's close by there's no sound and nothing's moving.

Her eyes close. It's not cold enough to shiver. But the sand is damp and she knows her skirt is getting wet. She rests the crystal in her lap, leans back on her hands and it's in this moment that she hears a tune, a snatch of music that comes and goes. A collapsed sigh like wind through tree tops, through a tangle of leaves and small branches. Except there are no trees. Just this eyrie flatness. She puts her head on one side, listens, breathing lightly until it comes again, subtle as gossamer, just a suggestion of sound, a melody inextricable from the emptiness. Impossible to tell whether it's a goatherd playing his lute somewhere over the dunes or whether it's in her head. As soon as she tries to work that out, it disappears, and try as she does, she cannot bring it back. It's only when her mind goes blank it returns. *There's music in silence if you can get still enough to listen.* She searches for the anger, knows it must be there somewhere, but for the moment its ferocity has been stolen by the gentleness of the night. She fills in the hole, surprised at the taste of salt on her fingers, sore and stinging from the digging. When she was little, her father would put bitter alum on them to stop her biting her nails. So she would tuck them away whenever she saw him. Perhaps she has done the same with her bities. Painted a wall around them to keep them safe. Are they ready yet, she wonders, to come out from behind that wall?

When finally she rises to walk back in the direction she came she knows finally that her time here has come to an end, but that it's a natural end, a line drawn underneath a final chapter and that when she leaves it will not be with regret. Or even anger. And that she is not leaving because of Dekker or Tay or Anna. Or for anyone but herself.

The sand on the rose is dry now. She blows at it and the petals separate. The crystal shimmers silver-blue in the moonlight.

It is well into the early hours of the next day when she walks in through the gates, the row of cabins on her left, the bare bulb still bright and burning above Tay's front door. Passing by, too tired to think of other than leaving the sand rose on his doorstep, she finds herself knocking once again, lightly this time, knuckles hollow on the metal; when she hears nothing, she watches her hand turning the handle, feels the thumping pulse of her heart in her throat.

The door swings open easily. She stands at the threshold for another moment, telling herself that she is surely trespassing, but just as assuredly she knows she is going in. *My door is always open to you. My door is always open.* Her mind moves slowly, slower than her sight to adjust to the fact that he is not sitting opposite in his usual chair, the skin around his eyes crinkling as she walks in.

'Tay. Taylor?' She calls out softly. Advances step by step through the small kitchen and around the partition into the bedroom. The bed not quite stripped, but it might as well be, covered as it is only by a too-thin sheet. Why has it taken so long to occur to her that he must be on nightshift, that of course he is on nightshift? It is only when she finds herself standing in the small bathroom, no towel on the rack, no toothbrush, toothpaste, soap, razor she understands that on this particular night he is not coming home. That perhaps he is never coming home.

But there is more than his absence here. The place, always sparsely occupied, is abandoned. She bends swiftly to the bottom cabinet, a half-used packet of Elastoplast and a bottle of aspirin tucked away in the corner. Moves into the bedroom, wrenches open the door of the cupboard, a pair of trousers, jeans, shirts neatly pressed, the brown *veldt* boots with the steel-capped toes.

TWENTY-EIGHT

When she comes to, she is sitting back against the metal wall of the cabin, hugging her knees to her chest, her head on her arms. In the same instant she recognizes she must have cried herself to sleep, that her clothes are damp and that she feels half-frozen, she senses she is not alone. She lifts her head to see Taylor standing in front of her, one hand on his heart, the other holding a battered brown suitcase.

'Gave me quite a turn, you did. What's up then?'

She rubs her eyes, passes her hands over her face. He's put the case down, but he still has his hand to his chest.

'What's the matter? With you? What's wrong?'

'B'n a long trip,' he says tiredly. 'I need the bathroom.'

She pushes her hair off her face. She goes to rise, realizes she still has the sand rose in her lap. She gets up slowly, places the crystal on the kitchen counter, moves automatically to make mugs of tea. It is still dark in his home, still before dawn; she will have time to get back before the camp awakes. By the time he reappears, the saucepan has boiled.

'If you didn't expect me to be here, why did you leave your door open?'

'Thought you might need a bolt hole. But not this time of night. You should be tucked up in bed asleep.'

'I didn't know you were going away.'

'No,' he agrees. 'You didn't. Settles himself in his chair, takes his mug from her. 'And neither did I until a few hours before I left.'

'You might have told me,' she mutters.

'How? Carrier pigeon?'

'Where did you go?

'Home.' He leans back into his chair, closes his eyes.

'Is. Everything all right?'

'Now. Now it is. Yes.'

She knows she should go. Put down her mug and leave. It is not the right time, she knows that, remembers her silent promise to herself to say nothing. But there's something in her stronger than pride.

'Why did you do it?'

'Do what?' The skin around his closed eyes tightens.

'Katya?' Exaggerates the syllables. Can't bring herself to say Kat.

'What about Katya?'

'She says.' She doesn't know how to phrase this. Tries out several phrases in her head. In the end says, 'You and her. This idea of the flat in London.'

'B'n checkin' up on me, have you?' His face still now, a stone wall.

'I ran into her. By accident…incident really. In the store. She invited me back. How could you?' Her voice muffled as she holds the steaming mug to her face, grips the counter. 'How could you.'

Eyes open now. Sets his unblinking gaze on her in the usual way, takes a long swig of his tea. His lips are tight.

'And there I was thinkin' that what I did with another consenting adult before meeting you was my business.'

'Before meeting me? What do you mean *before*?'

'That's old stuff. She went through a bit of turmoil years back. And I helped out, you might say. Surprised she's still on about it.'

'Years ago. You mean?'

'Years ago,' he repeats flatly.

'But.' She doesn't know where to look. 'All that stuff you said. You know, about being hard, feet of clay. All that. Isn't that what you meant?'

'What? Meant what?'

'Meant that. Oh heavens, you know what I mean.'

'I wish,' he says. 'I wish I did know what you mean. What I find upsetting is after all the time we've spent together, you think so little of me. The first person who suggests I'm cheating on you, you're ready to believe. Yes, there was a flat mentioned, I seem to remember. Back then. Her idea, not mine. In case you were wonderin'.'

'But why the feet of clay,' she says stubbornly. 'You said it, not me.'

'Uh, yes.' He leans back again, fingers together. 'Feet of clay. Thought with all your learnin' you might be familiar with the saying. Indicates weakness on the one hand, vulnerability, I suppose, on the other.'

'But how? I still don't understand. How is it applicable in this instance?' She shakes her head. Wants to do nothing more lay it down somewhere. To close her eyes. Stop her chattering mind. She's shivering and trembling both. Shaking so violently she has to clamp her back teeth.

He continues to look straight at her, his brow furrowed, the fingers of one hand moving slowly back and forth over his lips. 'Spell it out? If that's what you want though I wouldn't have thought it necessary. And it has nothing to do with Katya.

'You put me on a pedestal. And that's not fair. Because I'm a human being. Bound to fall off. That's what I meant. Do you need everything spelled out.'

'Yes.' She glares. 'I'm fed up with the bloody cryptic quizzes.'

'Nothing to tell that you don't already know. That has any importance.' He leans forward, his mug on his knee. 'But if you need reminding.

'I'm married, Dana. As you've known from the first. Made no secret of that. But what's always sat uneasily with me is being married and having my way with you at the same time. With nothing to offer in return. Clear about that, too, from the start. But it's not in me to turn down the offer of a beautiful woman. Same time, I will never leave my wife. Strange as it may seem, I'm pretty fond of the Lady Mary. B'n together a long time. Never dropped her bundle when there were plenty times she could've. Good mum to the kids. Held things together all these years. So I'm having my cake, as they say. And eatin' it too.

'Things that worry me about you. Your need for certainty, frantic search for affection. Tried to tell you how life doesn't work like that. That there are no certainties.

And affection dissolves like ice cream if you try to grasp it. Left with the stickiness and not much else. But I failed you there, too. Failed to get it across.'

She puts down her tea, grips the counter top with both hands. If only he had sighed, showed signs of irritation or if he'd looked away perhaps, or around or into the distance. Or even if he had brazenly tried to hold her gaze. Instead, fingers clenched now, mouth tight, he continues to stroke his lips, his chin. If he wasn't sitting in the chair and she pushed him – gently with her forefinger only – he would fall over.

She pushes herself away from the counter, lets her hair fall forward and combs it roughly with her fingers before she twists it back up, secures it with the pin. Smoothes her skirt with both hands and bends to scoop up her sandals.

'I'm leaving anyway,' she says. Her voice muffled, her gaze fixed now on the rose. 'Leaving the camp, that is. Going home myself.'

'Known that for a long time. Good choice. Pick up your life again.'

She wonders how he's known when she only knew for sure herself a few hours back, but he's already out of his chair to open the door. The light bounces in. He nods at the crystal on the counter.

'Nice one. Wherever you came across it. Don't leave that behind. In the old stories, desert roses spell good luck.'

'Yes,' she says. Moves out to face the lights snapping on around the compound. 'But it's already brought me luck.' She glances up at him briefly, smile twisted. 'I'm passing it on to you. It's your turn.'

She steps down onto the sand, braces herself for the sound of the door closing behind her, holds her head high and doesn't look back.

EPILOGUE

London

It was the scrape of pans hinting that supper was on its way that finally roused him.

He had no idea how long he had been sitting there. Only that the street light was shining through the window and that from the way the branches of the trees were carrying on, it was getting up to be an unpleasantly windy night.

He stood up, rubbed his arms, lifted the corner of the cloth he'd slung across the canvas. Switched on the light above it.

'So long. Kid. So long,' he said softly. Remembered murmuring those words once before. Standing in the doorway of his home, careless of the windows that were writing his story even as they lived their own, watching until she vanished into a gap between two houses.

Uh. He dropped the cloth, shook himself back to the autumn evening. Suddenly the inscription irritated him. *To my darling*. Too sentimental. Mary was right. It was unlike him and unnecessary altogether. The painting spoke for itself. He'd work on setting up another less maudlin mount in the morning.

In turning too quickly to snap off the light he knocked the jar of paint water from the counter, stooped to catch it inches from the floor.

Acknowledgements

My deepest thanks to Carol Major, consultant at the National Writers House of Varuna, for her enthusiasm and suggestions on an early draft of this novel. To Richard for his love and patience, his reading and re-reading of the final manuscript – and to Toni, Tammy and Viv for their unfailing encouragement and support.